Believe
Mel Teshco and Kylie Sheaffe

1

Believe

Cover Art by Helzcat Designs
https://www.helzkatdesigns.com/

Chapter One

Melbourne, Australia
   Cutting Edge Nightclub
   Saturday, March 12th

House music saturated the club as strobe lights flashed over the jam-packed dance floor, casting a smoky white haze over the churning mass of inebriated people below.

It'd been a hectic night, early morning now, though James was thankful to be kept busy at the bar. Serving beer, spirits, and wine had kept his mind side-tracked, his personal demons at bay.

Stevie had arrived a few hours earlier with three other friends, her sequined silver halter top and black mini-skirt revealing quite a bit more than it concealed.

He'd seen her dirty-dancing with her girlfriends and occasionally with other men at the very edge of the dance floor. She'd stayed as close to the bar, to him, as possible. With her come-on looks, pouty red lips and constantly tossed blond hair, she'd made it clear what she wanted.

Despite himself, he'd felt stirrings of need. She was a beautiful, willing woman. And it'd been a long time since he'd enjoyed a one-night stand.

"How's it going, mate?" Tom asked loudly, pulling up a bar stool before following James' gaze to where Stevie was shaking her booty. Tom grinned and leaned forward to shout, "She really likes you."

James shrugged and mouthed, "She likes a lot of men." *You should know,* he added silently.

Retrieving a glass from beneath the counter, he pulled Tom his usual beer before pushing the tall glass towards his friend and conceding aloud, "Besides, I'm more interested in a one-man type of woman these days."

Tom laughed. "Man, we only just get you loosened up and now you're talking about settling down?"

It was the drugs that loosened him. It was the drugs he was attracted to. And it was probably the drugs that saw him hang out with Tom in the first place.

Tom gave a wry shake of his head before taking a mouthful of his drink. "What's her name?"

James felt his chest tighten along with a reluctance to reveal Marina's name. It was as if announcing it would somehow sully her purity. He was almost relieved when he caught sight of Stevie as she cavorted her way towards them.

"Hi, Tom," she said loudly, her voice shrill against the music. Her eyes glittered as she swayed her hips to the beat, her arms weaving seductively above her head. She smiled, lowered her arms, and leaned over the bar, giving him full view of what was on offer. "And hi, James," she added huskily in his ear, caressing his jaw with a manicured hand.

For an infinitesimal beat, he stayed put, enjoying her touch, feeding off her aroused state. Then he was pulling away, angry at himself, angrier at her. He didn't play those games anymore. "Don't."

Her hand fell away as Tom gasped out laughter more cruel than humorous. Visibly collecting himself, Tom turned to Stevie and all but shouted, "Forget about James. He's in love with someone else."

Even under the dull lights behind the bar, James could see her eyes flash hurt and envy. Still, she managed to pull herself together enough to offer, "Then she's a lucky woman."

Tom raised a brow and turned back, peering over his glass at James with nothing short of an ironic grin. Tipping back the last of his drink, he said, "That remains to be seen."

As James automatically pulled Tom another beer, he was all too aware of the innuendo. Tom might appear disinterested in anything and anyone but himself, but he had a sharp mind when he cared to use it. He just might make a damn fine doctor one day. Then again, he could as easily find himself a career in the seedier side of business.

Tom knocked back another mouthful, leaned forward then asked, "Don't suppose you'd be interested in coming to another of my after-parties?"

James shook his head. "Thanks, but no thanks." He turned away as Stevie openly stared. He was uncomfortable with her infatuation. Working at a nightclub he was well used to women coming on to him. Stevie just seemed a little too keen. "Think I'll hit the sack," he added loudly.

Tom grinned, tapping the cigarette pack in his shirt pocket. "Why sleep when you can stay awake all night?"

Stevie giggled, clearly hearing most of the conversation as she turned to Tom and rested a hand on his shoulder. "I guess I won't be going home any time soon."

Tom turned towards her, his grin becoming a leer. "I certainly hope not."

James inwardly shook his head, distracted by other patrons thirsty for their drink.

As the club wound down and the last ditch bid for alcohol consumption went up, he had little time to dwell on it. Nor his steadily worsening headache, his dry mouth and eyes, along with a swollen tongue that brought on even greater need to quell the substance itch.

Tom reappeared at the bar as James was cleaning up, most of the partygoers reluctantly tromping out the exit doors. "I'm off now, mate," he said, the whites of his eyes tinged red, his stare glassy.

James nodded abstractedly, only too conscious now of the vicious squeeze behind his eyeballs and feeling almost resentful of Tom's high.

When his friend turned away, James blurted, "Wait." Oh, shit. "Could you do me a favor?"

"Say no more, my friend." Tom grinned knowingly as he plucked the cigarette pack from out of his pocket and placed it onto the bar. "You owe me one." With a wave that was more a salute, Tom disappeared through the last straggling throng of night-clubbers being shepherded towards the doors.

James hardly noticed. His eyes stayed glued to the packet for a long minute before he grabbed it and stuck it in his pants pocket. Sick with self-loathing, he was nevertheless champing at the bit to get home and seek mellow oblivion.

An hour later, sitting on the floor in the darkest corner of his lounge room, he took his first drag, absently aware of the tip flaring bright, the rough and bitter tasting smoke pulling down his throat. And finally, the creeping feeling of bliss.

He exhaled on a hacking cough, drowning out the faint, tinkling notes of a piano. "What are you doing up at this early hour, Marina?" he murmured, reflexively taking another drag before pulling a recliner to the window and contemplating the house next door.

His brow furrowed. Dawn light stroked the tin roof, giving off an unearthly silver aura. Marina's dog, Rocco, abruptly bolted around the corner, tongue lolling, the chain links on his collar giving off the same gleaming silver.

James leaned forward, alert and disbelieving at seeing who the dog was running towards. "Josie!" he breathed. "No. Bloody. Way."

The hospital wouldn't have released her, not yet. At least, not after her latest episode.

She raised her head, as if aware of him, her hand smoothing over the dog's fur-ruffled head. The silver aura encompassing her and the dog brightened sharply. The piano notes rose in a crescendo, impossibly loud. Then the haze disappeared, right along with Josie and the dog.

Oh, shit!

He woke with a start. His breath tore in and out of a dry, rasping throat as he opened gritty eyes to the sun's glare that came through his open curtains. His heart raced, his belly empty and gurgling. He felt like he'd been hit by a bus.

"Some nightmare," he muttered, shaking his head in disgust at seeing the stub of his joint still pressed between his fingers. "Why don't I just burn the house down while I'm at it?"

His cell phone chimed and he staggered to his feet, disorientated as he retrieved it from his pocket and answered almost vaguely. Wandering back to the window, he took his fill of Marina who was clipping an oversized shrub back into shape, Rocco dozing near her feet.

Unconsciously, he smiled. "Sorry, who is it?" he asked into the phone.

The professor patiently identified himself, and then proceeded to invite him over for lunch. James found himself agreeing, his gaze glued to Marina when he added, "Is there enough room for one more guest?"

A warm chuckle filled his ear, the professor agreeing immediately. Once James was told the Brighton street address, he disconnected, staring at Marina a little longer and frowning when the recent, weird dream intruded on his present preoccupation.

Damn, the vision of Josie and Rocco had felt so real, too real. Clearly it had been an aftereffect of the weed.

He raked an unsteady hand through his grimy hair. He grimaced, forcing his limbs into action. He couldn't ask Marina out somewhere looking like the contents of a dumpster and probably smelling even worse.

She'd seen him at his worst, knew he was anything but worthy of her. He wouldn't allow her to see him like that again.

After a hot shower, a shave, and a vigorous brushing of his furry teeth, then dressing in one of his favorite, more casual style of suits, he stepped outside.

The click-clicking of secateurs was loud in the still air, the traffic heading past the cul-de-sac a faint drone. Rocco sat up and whined. Marina turned, her hovering smile revealing her uncertainty.

His chest constricted. *Shit.* He couldn't blame her for holding the other night against him. Not one bit. He should never have gone over there in the state he'd been . . . he should never have been in that state to begin with. By doing so, he just may have lost all chance with Marina.

He cleared his throat. "I hope this isn't a bad time." Damn, he sounded like an idiot. He was an idiot!

"Of course not," she denied, reservation fairly oozing from her voice.

He swiped a hand over his burning eyes. "You're still mad at me after the other night." She didn't deny it, and misery ate at his guts like acid. So much for Marina coming to lunch with him, though that was the least of his concerns involving Marina right now. "I probably should go." He gave a jerky nod and turned away.

"James, wait."

He stilled, scarcely breathing. He slowly swung back to face her and she lifted a hand, palm up.

"I'm sorry for being rude, it's just—" Her hand dropped back to her side, bangles clanking. "—I have issues with people who use drugs. Big issues."

Oh, man. The muscles in his shoulders constricted, board-stiff. "Let me guess. The father of your baby was—"

"An addict. Yes." She sighed, dropping the secateurs to the ground and using the back of her hand to swipe hair off her damp brow. "Of course, he was good at acting normal, he had to be to hold on to his high-powered corporate job." Her eyes clouded. She shrugged, so much hurt in that one stiff little movement. "He needed to pay for his habit."

Breath hissed between James' teeth. "You must hate me right now."

She shook her head. "No! I could never hate you, James." She bit her bottom lip. Sighing, she admitted, "And therein lays the problem."

James nodded, guilt souring his gut. "You don't want to like me?"

"I don't want to like you quite this much. I can't," she qualified. "At least, not so soon." Her bottom lip wobbled and he watched her gnaw on it, keeping it still. "Seeing you high the other night really shocked me, and only reinforced my doubts."

She laid protective hands over her belly. "I have my baby to consider now, and I'll do whatever it takes to keep him, or her, away from that kind of life."

Oh, hell. What would she say if he told her about the joint he'd smoked earlier this morning, about the prescription and over-the-counter drugs he popped every day? He swallowed, feeling sweat sheen on his brow, dribbling between his shoulder blades and leaving him hotter under his suit collar than ever before.

He couldn't tell her. Not if it meant he'd lose her. Because suddenly, whole-heartedly, he couldn't lose her. Besides, he'd give up soon. He would.

He managed a nod. "I understand." Only too well.

"You do?" She cast him a doubtful look.

"Yes. Completely." He sank onto his haunches, picking up a branch cutting and rolling it between the palms of his hands. "I like you a lot, too, though my head tells me I shouldn't."

Marina stepped towards him, her twin bangles clanging together again as she put a hand on his shoulder. Warmth immediately seeped through his shirt, into his skin, delicious and tingling. So different than Stevie's touch.

"I can't imagine too many men who'd be attracted to me in my present condition," she said, as though that explained everything.

"Marina." His throat worked convulsively. He cleared it and muttered, "You're beautiful."

She smiled, glowing even with the doubts shadowing her stare. "Thank you."

Her hand lingered, and with the ensuing silence he found his other senses clamoring: the rasp of her blunt, uncolored nails dragging gently back and forth above his collarbone, the gentle swell of her belly beneath her daisy-yellow shirt, and the subtle, jasmine fragrance of her creamy skin.

She released him abruptly and stepped away, looking contrite and self-conscious. "Sorry. I'm sure you didn't come over to listen to my grievances. Ah, what did you come over for?"

"A friend of mine asked me over for lunch." He shrugged, feeling a little self-conscious too. "I took the liberty of asking if I could bring someone, you, along."

She chewed her lower lip, indecisive. A grin abruptly broke through, a pretty flush spreading across her lightly freckled cheeks. "Well, I haven't made any plans."

He grinned right back. "You'd like to come, then?"

"Yes. Yes, I think I would. Thank you." She glanced down at her clothes, swiping her hands across the seat of her pants. "I'll have to change."

"Of course, yes." Though she looked gorgeous just how she was. "Give me a yell when you're ready."

"Okay. On one condition." Her eyes held a mischievous glint.

"Yes?" Anything.

"I want you to change too, into something casual. I've never seen you in anything but a suit."

His stomach lurched but he managed a shrug. "Sure." But he was anything but sure. His suit was a part of him. Damn, it'd been so long since he'd gone without his . . . what? Formal armor? Outer shell? Bowheart shield?

Whatever. One thing was for certain. For Marina, he was certain he could slay at least one of his personal demons.

The drugs, he'd overcome that demon . . . later. As he spun around and strode back to his house, he realized he had a spring in his step that was almost jaunty.

James pressed the doorbell of the Newton's elegant brick veneer home, feeling ridiculously proud and nervous with Marina by his side.

He wanted to make a good impression. He wanted to show Marina the man he could be.

A barefooted Robyn opened the door. "James!" Her smile was welcoming and open. "It's so great to see you again."

The older woman stepped forward and pressed a kiss to his smooth-shaven cheek, before she turned to Marina. "And so nice to meet you . . .?"

"Marina," she said with a warm smile.

Robyn enfolded her into her arms for a brief, warm hug, but James saw her smile slip before she pulled away. The older woman quickly recovered her composure and said sincerely, "What a lovely name."

Marina's cheeks flushed pink. "Thank you."

James frowned a little, sensing an underlying tension in Robyn even as she said brightly, "Anytime, dear. And I'm so pleased you could come at such short notice."

"I'm glad you could have me," Marina returned graciously. She handed Robyn a bottle of red wine, shrugging, "I usually bring a dessert."

"Oh, aren't you a sweetheart!" Robyn accepted the gift as a sliding door swished open from the far end of the dining room. James craned his neck and grinned at the professor as he stepped inside from an expansive, terracotta-tiled patio, bringing with him a waft of frying meat and caramelized onions.

The professor strode forward to meet them. "You're just in time," he announced, sliding one arm around his wife with tongs still in hand and giving James a thumbs-up with his free hand. "Steak and rissoles are just about ready."

James' grin widened. "It smells delicious."

"I'm glad to hear it. Because this once I expect you to eat a whole lot." His eyes crinkled at the corners, revealing well-worn laugh lines. He turned to Marina, and James noted the slip in his expression when he took in her baby-bump. The professor quickly masked his reaction. "And this must be your friend?"

He nodded. "This is Marina."

Robyn stepped closer to her husband before she waved the guests inside. "Come through and get comfortable. There's a lovely breeze out the back so we thought it might be nice to sit at the patio outside."

Minutes later they were enjoying a barbecue lunch with all the trimmings: still-warm potato salad, coleslaw, and garden salad with generous dollops of homemade, tangy tomato chutney.

The professor leaned back with a contented sigh, hands patting his belly. One hand lifted to scrape over the stubble of his chin as he directed a look at James. "I must say Marina appears to be good for you, James. I've never seen you so relaxed."

"Why, thank you!" Grinning like a schoolboy, James scraped his chair back and stood. Lifting his arms, he slowly spun around, showing off his outfit of tan slacks and a red and cream striped polo shirt.

Marina burst into a fit of giggles, clapping her hands and cheering, "Looking good, James. Looking good!"

James returned to his seat, but not before Robyn shared a wry grin with her husband.

James' spirits lifted, warmth infusing him from the inside out. This was what a real family shared at the table. Love, laughter, joy.

As if in confirmation, Marina reached out and squeezed his hand, her cocoa-stare shimmering with appreciation.

His heart jerked into double-speed, his suddenly dry throat rendering him speechless.

The silence hovered, thick as treacle. Then a baby squalled somewhere nearby, starting up a rousing neighborhood chorus of yapping dogs.

Pushing out of her seat, Robyn tugged a wine bottle from its bucket of ice. Deftly uncorking it, she went to pour James a measure.

He put a hand over the glass. "Not for me, thanks. I don't drink."

Robyn withdrew the bottle. "Oh, I'm sorry. I didn't realize."

"Nothing to apologize about, you couldn't have known." He shrugged and conceded starkly, "My father's an alcoholic."

Robyn's face softened. "I'm sorry. But I'm so glad you've chosen a different path."

"My sentiments exactly," said the professor. "You've broken the link in the chain before the habit could be passed along."

Marina gave James' hand another squeeze before she glanced at Robyn and the half-tipped wine bottle still suspended in her hand. She shook her head and patted the swell of her belly. "None for me either, thanks." She swept a hand to encompass Robyn and her husband. "But, please, you two lucky things go ahead and enjoy it."

Robyn's face abruptly whitened. She swayed, and as her husband reached for her she choked out, "Please excuse me for a moment."

The wine bottle slipped from her hand, clanking onto the tabletop as Robyn reeled away, heading towards the sliding doors that led inside.

James turned to the professor, reading his stricken face perhaps a second before the older man managed to get rid of any hint of despair.

Marina pushed to her feet. "I'll go and check on her if that's okay."

Only when Marina had disappeared inside did the professor confess, "My wife and I have been blessed in every aspect of our lives, except our inability to have children." He shrugged. "IVF was our last hope, but Robyn miscarried for the third time just a few weeks ago."

Not so lucky after all.

The professor's pain emanated from him as though a dark cloud, and this once James had no idea what to do, what to say. "I'm so sorry. I had no idea," he said lamely.

The older man nodded. "It's not public knowledge. We've kept it private, for obvious reasons."

James nodded. "No one will hear anything on the matter from me. And Marina—"

"Is more than trustworthy." The professor smiled. "We would count ourselves lucky to have you as our friends."

"The feeling is more than mutual."

Ten or so minutes later, Marina and a much more composed Robyn, returned outside. The professor stood and pressed a kiss to his wife's cheek before murmuring in her ear, "Our time will come. You'll see. Keep the faith."

James was close enough to hear the reassurance, so why the sudden shiver of presentiment that shot down his spine?

The professor angled his head to include Marina in his warm stare as he said, "I'm glad you ladies came back. James was just telling me about his time in Africa. It's fascinating stuff, which I'm sure you both might like to hear."

"You've been to Africa?" Marina asked James, clearly fascinated.

James nodded. "Yes. My time there is what fired me up to become a doctor."

Robyn played with a napkin on the table. "Is that why you want to specialize in pediatric care?" She exchanged a look with her husband. "I was told about your intuitive knowledge that helped save a premature baby at the hospital."

Marina's eyes widened. "You did?"

James suddenly wished for his suit jacket and his tie, something to shield the flood of self-consciousness that hit as though a king tide rushing over dry ground. "The professor recognized the symptoms, too," James conceded. "It was just nice to be given the opportunity to prove myself."

"Despite the other doctors' disapproval and thoughts contrary to your diagnosis," Robyn's husband chuckled.

James raised a brow and said wryly, "That's about the gist of it."

"So, why Africa?" Robyn prompted. "It's one country my husband and I had planned to visit. The people. The wildlife." Her voice dropped. "The children."

James ignored Robyn's distress, knowing to show any sympathy might well push her over the edge. Instead he answered honestly. "To cut a long story short, I took a twelve-month hiatus from study and stayed in London with a barrister friend of my father's. I think my dad was hoping I'd be influenced by him and want to enter law." He shook his head. "He was a pompous jackass . . . I lasted a little over a week."

The professor's eyes gleamed with wry amusement. "So, in fact, it was your dad who turned the screw further against his own cause."

James nodded. "Yes."

"So why did you decide medicine?" Robyn asked, openly curious now and the pain in her eyes receding.

"Good question." Marina leaned forward in her chair, an elbow propped on the table, her chin in her palm.

"It all started when I was at an incredibly dull shindig in London. It was only after I began a conversation with a man who seemed even less inclined than me to be there, that the party got interesting."

"Go on," said Marina, seemingly hanging on to his every word.

James took a sip of water. "David, Doctor Lowe, worked on a mostly voluntary basis for a children's organization.

He wanted to make a difference, and he did." James spread his hands. "Coming from an altruistic family, I found his principles, his core beliefs, his passion, remarkable."

Robyn balled the napkin in her hands. "So he convinced you to fly to Africa as a volunteer?"

James nodded. "I didn't need to be coaxed. It seemed almost as if fate had stepped in and made the decision for me. And I never once regretted going to Africa and giving law a wide berth."

The older James covered Robyn's hand. "How did Africa's pediatric care measure up?"

James ran outspread fingers through his hair, causing the ends to bristle. "Doctor Lowe travelled to villages where there was very little outside medical influence. Malaria was widespread, causing many premature and underweight births." He shook his head. "There were no humidicribs and yet, some of these babies thrived who were held close to their mother's, kept warm by breast milk on demand and skin-to-skin contact."

Marina leaned forward. "But surely the pregnant women had doctors, someone to deliver their babies?"

James shook his head. "Not where we went. Though some of the witchdoctors I saw were uncanny with their ancient ways. I believe they saved some babies that Western medicine might not have."

"Fascinating stuff," said the professor, his eyes alert. "I've actually made similar observations as well as many other unscientific happenings over the years," he conceded.

"I can vouch for that," Robyn agreed. "I'm almost certain his journal has been made fat with ink."

James poured water out of a jug in the center of the table, topping up Marina's glass. "I'd love to see it one day."

The professor smiled. "I'd be only too happy for you to read it. I'd like to hear your opinions on some of the unexplainable events I've noted."

Robyn stood, not quite the smiling hostess but as close to normal as one could expect after her emotional turmoil. "Anyone for coffee?"

James came to his feet. "No, thanks." He swept a look at Marina. "If it's okay, I was thinking of calling in on my sister before we head home."

Marina stood. "I'd like that."

"Oh, you have a sister?" Robyn asked. "You two must bring her next visit."

James didn't reply, it was all he could do not to reject such an idea. It was Marina who stepped in and said, "You'd love Josie. She's an angel."

James couldn't remember the last time he'd felt so at ease, so content. He might have inwardly hyperventilated at the idea of bringing Josie to meet the Professor and Robyn, but with Marina as company even that anxiety had melted away.

He only wished he could have eased the older couple's distress as easily.

When he pulled the BMW into the Karlcodi car park a little over half an hour later, there were only desultory-like tendrils of dread groping at the pit of his belly.

He swung open Marina's door and as she climbed out with her eyes shining with concern, she asked, "Are you okay?"

He pushed the passenger door shut and said truthfully, "Yes."

"I'm glad."

He took her hand in his, acting a love-struck fool with a grin splitting his face, but caring less. He'd never once cracked a genuine smile on Karlcodi grounds, and he wasn't about to wipe the humor off his dial now. Not deliberately.

Tess was at the nurses' station when, hand-in-hand, he and Marina pushed open the hospital's front door.

James' smile dropped only fractionally when Tess saw them, her face tightening.

She nodded stiffly before informing them in a polite tone, "Josie is back in her room and doing well."

"Is she medicated?" he asked, wondering what state they'd find her in.

"Yes. Thanks to your tip-off the doctor has made doubly sure her medication is being administered as it should."

His smile abruptly wilted. What had he done? He blew out a breath. Josie would never forgive him if she figured out he was the one who'd informed the staff about her not taking her meds.

He nodded. "Thanks, Tess. I'll go check on my sister."

They found her standing at the barred window. Her back to them and her arms crossed at her waist, Josie rocked gently side-to-side, humming tunelessly.

He swung a look at Marina. She nodded at him, but stayed by the door to give him a moment with his sister.

"Josie."

Her humming ceased. She stilled and then slowly turned to face him. Her expression was somber, yet blanked out somehow, as though everything she was feeling ceased to exist.

"James." She took a step forward but didn't touch him. "I can't see Molly anymore. I can't see . . . anyone."

That was a good thing, wasn't it? The medical staff was ensuring she took her drugs, and this was likely the result. So why did his victory feel like her loss?

He drew her into his arms, but she remained stiff, unyielding. "Come on," he said gently, and turned to lead her over to the bed. "How about I read you a poem? You'd like that, wouldn't you?"

Josie sat onto the bed, prim and proper just like their mother had taught her. She lifted her head and said, "I'd like Marina to read it."

"Oh, I would love to, sweetie." Closing the door behind her, Marina plucked the poetry book from the bedside table, then sat on the floral chair in the corner before flipping the book open. "Which one would you like me to read?"

Josie's head tilted to the side. "Whichever one is in front of you now."

Marina smiled. "Fair enough." Clearing her throat she looked down and started to read.

I remember it all . . .

Looking down upon my body

Flapping, I squirm in crumpled scraps of steel

Dug into soft earth, a burrow no—a furrow.

Dragged screaming from the bitumen, crushed, speared, my past reappeared—

I do believe . . .

This is real. No nightmare, no garish dream, from which I wake with stifled scream . . .
I remember it all . . .
The panic dancing in my brain
Chest impaled with sudden fear, gagging on the searing pain
Rebirth, thrown shrieking from my plastic womb,
Regurgitated, spewed into the shattered soil,
I quietly choke on roots, coiled around my broken fingers,
My nails, chunks torn away—seen through soil-burdened lashes . . .
I do believe . . .
This is my tomb."
~Sue Allen

Chapter Two

Josie's spark of pleasure immediately dimmed as Marina's lilting voice read the poetic words. She wanted to scream, wanted to block out the sound of the story unfolding, which replicated too closely her recent vision.

Only, she couldn't speak through the sudden restriction of her throat, couldn't voice her fears, her growing horror at the very thought of her brother's death. And she felt herself slowly drowning in a sea of anguish.

At some point she'd started rocking back and forth, the only sound to push past her throat a tuneless humming that overrode at least some of the crazy-real words.

Marina's voice faded into silence as she raised her head. Returning the book to the bedside table, Josie was aware of the uneasy look she gave James.

She inwardly flinched. How she loathed those silent exchanges, where people assumed her mental state rendered her blind. Mostly she was even more aware, more attuned to what was around her. And yet it only made her feel more alone, more of an outcast. How she wished the manual transmission in her brain, too often stuck in gear, was automatic like everyone else's.

She wished right then she could weep, allow tears to cleanse her soul and ease the emotional torrent building within. But she couldn't cry, and panic escalated, her throat thickening, leaving her choked up. Useless. And barely able to draw breath.

"Josie, are you okay?" Marina asked softly.

Josie pretended not to hear. It was easier that way, easier than trying to voice her fears and having to deal with the fallout. Besides, if she did speak it would make it all too real, and it'd be her fault . . . again.

Right now it was easier to focus on her breathing . . . her sanity.

And then it happened.

A sudden, oppressive darkness filled the room, a bleak shadow materializing into frightening life before her. Her eyes widened, fixing on the man whose energy swirled with sickening darkness. Her throat suddenly loosened as every other part of her body went taut with shock. "Who are you? What do you want?" A sob tore from her throat. "Where's Molly?"

Marina's voice seemingly floated now, abstract and somehow less real than this dark apparition. "We want to help you, Josie. We don't know where Molly is."

Then James put a hand on Marina's forearm and shook his head, signaling Marina to be quiet.

He was seeing it, too, Josie realized. Though she couldn't tear her gaze away from the specter, she could still make out the horror in her brother's eyes, see the disbelief on his whitening face as he stared at the man.

Like an intravenous drip, his fear fed her own, adding to the emotional carnage heaving within.

"No!" She shook her head. "I want Molly," she shrieked, "I don't want you!"

Then a name sounded in her mind, over and over. Sarah Jane. Sarah Jane.

A startling, horrific vision of a young woman's dead, mutilated body simultaneously filled Josie's head, violating yet another of her senses. When her shriek pitched into an unearthly, high-pitched scream, the dark, shadowy stranger abruptly moved towards her.

The shadow stooped to her level and she gulped in a breath, shuddering into silence. Heaven help her, his eyes might be devoid of all humanity, but they filled her with his pain, his anguish, his hell, until his suffering became hers.

She shook her head harder, denying him the help he demanded. Pressing backward until her shoulder blades thudded against the wall, she sucked in another horrified breath and screamed hoarsely, "Get away from me."

A vision abruptly filled her head: the stranger before her, now with a noose around his neck. Hanging. Dead.

And in that instant, Josie's disorientated emotions shifted into lucid understanding. This man had ended his life to be free, but instead he'd become trapped in an ether world of his own making.

With crystal clarity she knew that until she helped him, he'd overshadow Molly, making it impossible to see or hear her.

His unfinished business had just become hers.

Dragging her knees to her chest and anchoring them with her arms, her tight throat humming a discordant and fierce tune, Josie squeezed her eyes closed and began rocking faster. But she was unable to block out his presence, unable to retreat into herself.

The door abruptly swung open. And even with the frightening emotions crowding inside her, she didn't need to open her eyes to know Doctor Leonard had shambled into the room. Through the fog of her gathering horror she could hear the approach of his heavy tread, sense his intimidating air long before he boomed, "What's going on with my patient?"

Don't pretend you care now.

There'd be no help from him. He'd prescribe more drugs, making her even more susceptible to this dark side she didn't want to see. The medication may have at first numbed her to everything, not now. It had changed everything . . . changed her perceptions, her clarity of mind. The doctor moved towards her and clasped her wrists with his meaty hands. "Who are you talking to, Josie?"

She forced her eyes open, only to see the stranger's shadow pass through the doctor, before superimposing over him. The specter's wispy hands curled around her forearms, sending prickles of ice-cold revulsion up her spine.

"Don't touch me." She stared at the dark silhouette of the stranger, adding hoarsely, "Murderer!"

The doctor dropped her wrists like she'd singed his fingers, but Josie scarcely cared. The stranger hadn't removed his grip from her arms and his eyes held hers, wholly hypnotic and compelling.

"Where's Molly?" she hissed.

Then, as suddenly as the stranger had come, he dissolved, taking his emotions with him and leaving her feeling drained and washed out. Empty.

The doctor stood with his hands on his hips, not an ounce of give in his expression as he asked brusquely, "Talk to me, Josie. Tell me who you saw, what you heard?"

All mandatory questions for the doc to note down later. And yet suddenly she wanted to talk, felt compelled to answer. "A murderer came to me," she said in a thin, hoarse voice. "I know where his victim is buried."

The doctor raised a gray brow. But she didn't fail to see his fleshy lips compress, his jaw tighten. He cleared his throat. "Oh?"

"Yes." She looked straight at him now, suddenly unafraid, suddenly aware how frightened Doctor Leonard had become underneath his oversized body. "A young girl with a butterfly-shaped birthmark on her shoulder." As his nostrils flared, his eyes widening, she said softly, "Sarah Jane."

The doctor's face leeched of all color. He took a step backward, then another. Without a word he wheeled around and headed to the door, escaping through it with the speed of a much lighter man.

"How could you, Josie?" James asked, his voice rough with emotion.

She turned to him, uneasy and wretched even with her sanity restored and intact. "What?"

"Don't tell me you didn't know," James rasped. "It was all over the news. Doctor Leonard's daughter went missing four years ago, presumed dead . . . murdered. Everyone knew about her birthmark, the police hoped it'd help identify her by going public with her appearance."

Josie shrank a little, but it was all on the inside. "I didn't know," she whispered. She held his gaze. "I never watch the news." To do so brought on too many visions, more than she could handle. "Surely you don't think I was making it up?" Her eyes narrowed. "You saw the man in this room earlier, too. Didn't you?"

James' face tightened, his voice suddenly too much like their father's as he said, "Just because you think you see something, it doesn't mean you have to tell anyone. It's inappropriate and rude and—"

"James, please." Marina put a hand on his arm. "Don't you think Josie needs to speak her mind?" Her face was all gentle and loving as she added, "And to be honest, I didn't know anything about the doctor's missing daughter either." She shrugged. "I don't watch a lot of television. I'm usually listening to music or playing piano."

James pushed a shaky hand through his hair. "You might be right. But it doesn't give Josie reason to blurt out whatever she sees. If she really is so sensitive to people's emotions, she should know better than to bulldoze them with her visions."

Stop talking about me like I'm not even here!

He paced back and forth. "Something has to be done." He stared at Josie as though appalled by a sudden thought. "I'm taking your poetry book."

Josie froze, mute and disbelieving. How could he do that to her?

Marina frowned. "James, I'm not sure that is such a good idea."

James retrieved the book and held it to his chest, his gaze unwavering on Josie. "I'm sorry, Josie. I thought this book was good for you, now I'm not so sure."

Marina trailed beside James as he strode with a ramrod-stiff gait towards the door, her red-gold hair so vivid against his casual shirt. But Josie knew her brother's sudden preference for casual attire couldn't hide his hereditary traits. He'd never acted more like their Bowheart parents.

Marina shivered a little as they walked along the Karlcodi corridor towards the exit, silence heavy behind them.

James' granite expression gave nothing away, though she was only too aware of his simmering emotions. In that moment Josie's cherished poetry book seemed almost obscene in his clasp.

She wanted to back James up on his decision to take away Josie's book, but it didn't sit right with her. Not one bit. His sister didn't need punishment; she needed love and support. And right now James' way of thinking reflected a 'cruel to be kind' attitude Marina found disturbing.

Was that how the Bowheart children had been brought up? James opened the door for her and once outside, Marina sucked in the crisp, late-afternoon air.

A frog croaked, sending a couple of others into chorus. A plane droned high overhead as a gardener raked up papery leaves with a *swish-swish* sound beside a stately row of ruby-red roses.

How normal things seemed out here. As though what went on behind Karlcodi's closed doors was just another fragmented dream already becoming lost amongst the flotsam of her thoughts.

Little wonder James and Josie were so affected. There were things going on inside Karlcodi's walls she felt certain wouldn't be visible or experienced by anyone but the most attuned.

She stopped beside the gardener, her one arm outstretching until James stilled just ahead, her hand interlaced with his. She breathed in the heavily perfumed air, welcoming the balm to her senses after such turmoil. "How beautiful," she said, admiring the large blooms that were already tightening into fist-size buds.

"That they are," the gardener agreed in his faintly accented voice. He swept a hand to where a rectangular rock with gleaming plaque lay embedded into the ground, amidst the thorny rose stems. "No doubt watched over by the late Timothy Doore."

James stepped back, drawing her close to his side as though made protective by the news.

She gave him a tentative smile, unsuccessfully ignoring the delicious thrill of his touch as she refocused on the gardener. "I'm sorry. Did he . . . Timothy, die recently?"

The gardener removed his cap and held it to his chest with a wizened, openly disrespectful grin that showed a set of discolored, stumpy teeth. "Ay, he did. Went and 'ung himself. No one knows why."

She felt James stiffen beside her and perceived he, too, felt a bleak chill in the pit of his stomach. Her stare rested momentarily on the plaque. "How awful."

The gardener leaned on his rake, nodding. "He left no note, no nuttin'." As if imparting a great secret, he said, "He should never 'ave been released from Karlcodi." Leaning closer still, he added, "He should 'ave stayed a patient here instead of taking on the position of gardener on account of his fondness for plants."

Minutes later, the silence in the car grew almost deafening. James was clearly deep in thought, her own thoughts vacillating between Josie and what the gardener had said about the suicide of a former patient.

"I wonder where they found Timothy's body," she murmured. And when James glanced over, she added, "I have the weirdest feeling he hung himself somewhere at the hospital."

James blew out a breath. "I seriously hope not. That place doesn't need to add to its creep factor."

"Something spooked you today, didn't it?"

His hands clamped harder on the steering wheel. "Honestly, yes." His jaw tightened. "But just what it was that spooked me, I'm not entirely sure."

He stopped in his driveway and cut the ignition. Alighting, he strode around the car and opened her door.

She climbed out, feeling so ungainly now with her belly seemingly growing an inch every day. "Come over to my house for a coffee, and we can talk about it," she offered.

He opened the back door and retrieved Josie's poetry book. He straightened, so very handsome in his casual striped polo shirt with his hair not quite perfectly groomed. "I wish I could," he said, his voice on one hand registering regret, the other relief. "But I'm already late for my shift at the club."

She smiled. "Well, thank you for inviting me out today. The professor and Robyn are lovely."

"Yes. I'm only sorry the day ended like it did." He looked down at the book, as if seeing it for the very first time. He grimaced. "Would you mind looking after this, at least for a little while? I don't think I can bear having it right now."

"Of course." She took hold of the book, her free hand sliding up and down James' forearm as she added gently, "I'm here if, when, you want to talk."

He nodded, but she felt the distance suddenly grow between them. "Thank you." He sighed. "I should go."

"Of course." She dropped his arm and clutched the book to her chest, feeling her smile dissolve as she watched James stride inside as though he couldn't get away fast enough.

She knew something wasn't quite right with him, knew he was hiding things from her. Fool she might be, but somehow she didn't much care. Underneath it all, James was a good and noble man.

He just had to find himself.

The baby kicked, as if in agreement. And suddenly she didn't much feel like frowning anymore. She liked James, a lot, and she wasn't about to allow the bitterness and mistrust from her old relationship to taint things between them. Not anymore.

Rocco greeted her at the door with his tail whipping the air. "Good boy." She bent to scratch behind his floppy ears, smiling at the unashamed devotion shining from his chocolate eyes.

His claws *click-clicked* on the wooden floor as he followed her into the dining room, where her violin case lay on the wooden table, her treasured instrument cradled within.

She unclipped the case and ran her hand along the gleaming wood, over the now invisible crack, which had ran from the treble F hole to the purfling at the chinrest. She'd had it professionally mended with hide glue and reinforced with hardwood cleats.

Josie would be happy to know the violin was good as new.

She shook her head as she pulled up the nearest chair and sat, Rocco pushing his way under the table and flopping onto his belly with a doggy sigh. In all the chaos at Karlcodi she'd completely forgotten to mention this bit of good news to Josie.

She lifted a foot and massaged Rocco's back. Abstractedly she spread the poetry book open and, squinting at the title, she raised a brow and murmured, "Interesting."

On darkest days,
I find no solace in the laughter of friends, which never ends.
Their voices babble,
Somewhere on the outer edge—the jaw-dropping crumbling ledge,
Of insanity—a hollow chasm viewed within hate—
The rim on which my temper grates, maliciously . . .
When hours are gray, in place of song, my dreary darkness echoes long
And drags a steely coil of rope upon the vibrant music notes,
Which lay—
Silent . . .
Tombstones in my mind . . .
Leave me alone.
Cast me adrift.
Let me feed upon this conscious rift

I've driven like a stake into the iron ground
There is no sound.
Lightest are the days when music dwells within me,
When every sound sings me a personal tune,
In every room or out among the trees—
I treasure days such as these, when gnashing teeth, celebrate rhythm—
Syncopated molars are as good for the soul as any sip of honeyed wine—
That bumptious need to feed the rhythm,
God given, chew in time, chew in time . . .
Let me play my violin, make it sing,
Draw the bow across the string with deep resonance,
Quiver in my spine, feel the music, make it mine—
Dancing in staccato bursts, fingers racing, tapping tight, their very tips upon the wires—
Pattering, taking flight, the semi quavers racing higher, higher, higher still,
Until—
The zenith of the music flows and soars and crests again!
Forgotten is the dreary pain
Of loss and grief—
All of it is lost beneath the clarity of song,
And I linger long
On my pedestal of dreams—
Orchestral reams filling my heart and my mind,
As only human kind
Could ever understand—
Hand in hand . . .
My violin, my soul . . . intertwined, whole . . ."
~Sue Allen

Marina shut the book, feeling almost giddy with enlightenment. It was as though these words had removed her blinkers and compelled her to see what she had to do.

Dialing the local taxi service, she ordered immediate pick up. Hanging up, she drifted to her dining window and gazed out at the darkening indigo sky with its bloodshot horizon, waiting until she saw James slip outside some ten minutes later.

She couldn't put her finger on it, but something about him was different. It wasn't his change of clothes. It was his walk . . . he moved like an automaton. Even from the distance she could see his expression was cold. Unfeeling.

She bit her bottom lip and watched through the slatted blinds as he reversed out the driveway, his profile angled away from her house.

Hiding something?

No matter how strong her attraction to James, how much her intuition compelled her to be with him, if being part of his life meant stepping off the straight and narrow path she'd chosen for her baby, then there'd be no future with him.

Just thinking about that possible scenario caused an ache in her chest.

Taking a deep breath, she released the blinds, and as they snapped back into place it was as if a door snapped over her bleak thoughts.

Josie needed her now.

It was probably best James didn't know she was going back to see his sister. She turned from the window and lifted her chin. She didn't need his permission to help out a friend.

No sooner had James driven down the road, she heard the taxi pull into her driveway.

Rocco growled and then whined fretfully.

"It's okay," she said, but a little frisson of fear slipping down her spine had her reconsider. She lifted the blinds again, double-checking it really was her taxi she'd heard. Double-checking that it really had been her imagination working overtime and not something all too real.

So stupid really, but lately she couldn't shake the feeling someone was watching her . . . following her?

As if on cue, something moved in the shadows cast by a group of trees near her boundary fence, opposite James' house.

Her heart jumped and she let out a choked scream. The blinds dropped. Almost simultaneously, the taxi horn sounded. When she next forced herself to lift the blinds and look out, whatever had been there was gone.

All a figment of her overactive imagination, which had clearly been whipped up since her visit to Karlcodi.

With a shaky laugh, she made sure Rocco's doggy-door wasn't locked, then retrieved her violin in its case and made her way to the waiting car.

Anticipation fired through her bloodstream as she climbed into the taxi. Hopefully giving Josie this violin would make up for the loss of her poetry book.

The hospital loomed through the dusk shadows, its bulk rising upwards like a huge ship through the fog.

The driver swung the taxi around the car park. And as the headlights swept over the stately row of roses, the gardener's words immediately echoed in her head, no doubt watched over by the late Timothy Doore.

She shivered. There was a darkness here that penetrated the mind, an uneasy feeling of ill will, which susceptible visitors would undoubtedly blame on the aura of madness behind Karlcodi's walls.

Opening her purse, Marina gave the driver his fare and organized his return within the hour. Only after she stood watching the taxi's taillights retreat back down the driveway did she question what time visiting hours finished.

Tess was busy with paperwork when Marina approached the nurses' station close to the entrance doors. On seeing Marina, she glanced sharply at the wall clock. "Visiting hours finished half an hour ago."

Marina let out a sigh. "Really? To be honest, it hadn't even occurred to me until after I was dropped off." She hoisted the violin case to draw Tess' attention. "Coming back was kind of a spur-of-the-moment thing. All I could think about was bringing Josie a present and cheering her up."

Tess gave a stiff nod. "Yes, well, she could certainly use some kindness right now." She clucked her tongue. "That poetry book of hers was like her best friend."

"You knew James took it from her?" she asked, surprised Tess had noticed it gone.

"It never leaves her side." Tess' eyes widened, as though suddenly comprehending Marina's last sentence. "James took it away from his sister?" At Marina's nod, she said, "Josie hasn't said a word since I started my shift. I assumed her doctor had confiscated it." Her eyes narrowed thoughtfully. "Even the doc doesn't seem himself today."

Marina gripped the case a little tighter. "Josie upset him," she admitted. "She was having a vision when the doctor checked in on her. And she mentioned his deceased daughter."

"Oh, my." Tess abandoned her station and all her paperwork to draw Marina alongside her as she pushed through the doors and into the corridor beyond. "To tell you the truth, nothing surprises me too much anymore. There's more to this hospital than meets the eye."

"Oh?"

Tess' laugh wasn't joyful. "I wouldn't know where to start. But what I can tell you is that most of the nurses here have their own stories to tell, especially where Josie is concerned."

"I believe you," Marina said. At Tess' look, she added, "My aunt is a respected clairvoyant. Odd things are acceptable in my family."

"Still, you didn't hear anything from my lips," Tess said, stopping beside Josie's room.

Marina stilled. "Hear what?" she asked with a little smile.

Tess' face relaxed, and Marina felt a comradeship with her just then that overrode any hint of jealousy she'd felt earlier.

The nurse cleared her throat. "Make this a quick visit, won't you? It's against hospital policy for me to allow Josie any visitors at this time."

"I won't be long," Marina agreed. "I'll give her the violin, and get going."

Tess nodded, her voice becoming crisp. "Just make sure she stays in her room. Oh, and if she gets irritable or aggressive, terminate your visit immediately and report to me or one of the staff."

Marina wilted a little inside. What was she doing here? This was beyond her experience, her abilities. But a surge of confidence filled her as she recalled Josie's gentle approach with the magpie in James' front yard.

She might only have met Josie, but Marina knew she was a beautiful person inside and out, incapable of deliberately hurting anyone. "I will."

Tess glanced through the door's glass plate window to check on Josie. Apparently satisfied, she turned back to Marina. "Right. Well, I guess I'll leave you to it." About to swing away, the nurse hesitated, her freckled nose crinkling. "Just be warned. Josie may not be able to keep the violin. The doctor might decide it's unsuitable."

"Well, I only hope Josie gets a chance to prove to the doctor the violin is an instrument of beauty, not violence."

"Have you heard her play?" Tess asked.

Marina smiled, feeling suddenly warm in this place of dank coldness. "Yes. She played the violin for the first time ever only days ago. She was amazing . . . a music prodigy. I only hope you get a chance to hear her for yourself."

When Tess went off to do her rounds, Marina took a deep breath before pushing open the door to Josie's room, only to find her lying in her bed asleep.

But it was no dreamless slumber. The bedcovers appeared as though they'd been thrashed by nightmares, Josie even now murmuring something unintelligible in her sleep, her brow and hairline damp with sweat.

Marina put the instrument case down. "Oh, Josie." She moved forward, placing a hand on Josie's shoulder to gently shake her awake.

Josie's eyes flicked open. She gasped and shot into a sitting position. She shook her head, sobbing, "James can't die."

Marina inwardly reeled. She swallowed back the sudden bout of nausea, resting a hand on her belly as she said, "Josie, what did you see?"

"James . . . I saw James." She sucked in a breath. "James Edward, blue splattered red." She started to rock, her shoulders shaking. "Murdered by the man with a scar on his face."

Josie abruptly stopped rocking and looked straight at her, seemingly rational now even as Marina sank into emotional upheaval. "He knows you," Josie said with eerie assurance. "Yes, he has your photo." Her mouth firmed. "He broke it, though."

Marina shriveled inside, clutching her belly protectively as her mind screamed the truth. But she had to ask, had to make certain. "What does this man's scar look like?"

"You should know," said Josie, almost bewildered by Marina's apparent ignorance. "He has a zipper scar to keep his evil inside."

Marina breathed, slow and deep. She couldn't lose it now. Josie had a gift, and she wasn't about to throw it in her face with denial because she couldn't handle the truth. "You're right," she managed. "He hides his cruelty somewhere deep inside, but sometimes it leaks out." She gritted her teeth. "We have to keep James safe."

Josie shivered, conceding, "Only you can do that."

"What . . . how?"

"Molly can't help us, not right now." Josie shook her head, clearly fighting to stay out of her own hellish world, and losing. "Not while the murderer walks in her place, expecting my help."

"What does he seek?" Marina asked, somehow compelled to ask.

Josie rocked harder, rubbing her hands up and down her forearms as though chilled right through. "He seeks forgiveness."

"That's a big responsibility for a young woman," Marina said softly. She couldn't even imagine the huge burden on Josie's narrow shoulders right then.

Josie didn't appear to hear her as she continued rocking, now humming tunelessly.

She sat beside Josie on the bed. "Perhaps this will take your mind off things?" It was only when she placed the music case on the bed and unclipped the lid, that Josie stilled, silent but alert.

Like a butterfly climbing from its cocoon, Marina watched the transformation of frightened little girl to joyous woman.

"It's yours," Marina said, tearing up a little at Josie's obvious change.

"It is . . . really?" Josie's eyes were alight with wild hope. At Marina's nod, she took out the violin, almost reverently running her fingers along its delicate frame. "You've had it fixed."

"Yes."

"And it's really all mine?" she asked again, already forgetting about the fact she broke it in the awe of being its owner.

"Really truly," Marina said with a smile. "I want you to enjoy it, and practice your music whenever the fancy takes you."

"But it's not even my birthday."

"I don't need a birthday for an excuse to give a good friend a present."

Josie sat cross-legged on the bed, her radiance and joy infectious as she stared and stared at the violin.

"I'll leave you to enjoy it," Marina said. But of course Josie didn't hear or acknowledge her just then. All her focus was wrapped in her instrument.

Marina shut the door behind her and leaned against the wall nearby. Eyes closed, her head back, she soaked in the first wafts of music filling the air.

Though the sound wasn't the pure perfection of a master violinist, there was a raw quality and passion to the notes that was exquisitely beautiful and soulful.

"Wow, I see what you mean," Tess said with a grin almost splitting her face as she walked by. A male patient in a bright purple dressing gown shuffled alongside Tess, smiled dreamily, beatifically.

Marina stayed another few minutes, aware of the energy shift in the air. She could feel the music lift the bleakness, leaching the negative vibrations from the soul of the hospital, note by note.

She only wished the fear tightening like a fist in her chest at the thought of James' imminent death . . . murder, could as easily be expelled.

She shook her head. This sense of impending doom would be exactly what her ex-husband would want. Behind his zipper scar and flash suits, he really was a cold-hearted monster.

Another gust of music filled the air, and this time the sound really did chase away her anxieties. She was a strong, capable woman. And she believed James' time was not yet near. He had a lot of living to do yet, a lot of people to touch.

Walking down Karlcodi's corridor towards the exit, Marina was aware of the spring in her step. She blew the bangs off her brow with an elated breath. She'd been so right to trust her instincts.

Chapter Three

Carlton, Australia

Monday, March 14th

Rocco's plumed yellow tail swished from side-to-side as Marina poured his breakfast of doggy biscuits into his bowl. She slid a hand along his silky head. "Eat up, boy. We might get to go for a walk later."

A knock sounded on her front door. Somehow she knew it was James, but even so a little thrill shot through her body as she swung open the door and saw him standing there.

"Hi." She gestured for him to come inside, noting how handsome he was even with the shade of weariness he wore upon his face. "Is everything okay?"

He nodded and stepped inside. "Yes." He raked a hand through his hair and with a wry smile added, "A little tired from working last night, but I'll survive."

No doubt exacerbated by thoughts of his sister.

She shut the door behind him and asked, "Why don't you sit down and I'll make us some breakfast? If you're not in a hurry of course."

"Sure, thanks. That sounds good."

She smiled, feeling decidedly domestic as she gathered the ingredients for a pancake mixture. She watched as James took a seat at the table and leaned down, tapping a hand on his leg to encourage Rocco closer.

Rocco grinned his happy doggy grin, his claws clicking on the hardwood floor as he trotted straight over.

James ran a hand over the dog's head, pausing the moment his hand brushed along Rocco's neck. "Leather," he muttered, staring at his collar. "What happened to his link chain?"

Marina added a generous splash of milk to the bowl of dry ingredients. Cracking in an egg, she said, "He's never had a link collar, only the leather one he has on now."

"Oh."

Stirring the mix, she paused to ask, "What made you think he did?"

And why was it so important?

"Sorry, it's nothing. My mistake." He smiled, but it was filled with uncertainty. "I must have been seeing things."

Interesting. Was that a Freudian slip of the tongue or was there more to it than met the eye?

She kept the thought to herself as she lit the gas stove. Heating a fry pan, she added a dollop of butter and watched it quickly melt with a sizzle before she dropped in a ladle of pancake mixture. Lifting the pan to distribute the mix evenly over its base, she placed it back onto the heat.

"I'm not working today," he said into the silence. "And actually, it's the reason I came over this morning."

"Oh?"

"I wondered if you might be interested in seeing Green Moss Falls with me."

A piercing need surged within, and it had nothing to do with the exquisite beauty she imagined falls with such a name would offer. "Thank you. I'd like that."

She saw his jaw relax and realized he'd yet to perceive how much she wanted, despite some misgivings, to spend every moment possible with him.

Thoughtful, she lifted the pancake with a spatula and with a deft flip allowed it to cook on the other side. "I have a couple of things to do this morning first, though, if the afternoon would suit you?"

He nodded. "Sounds like a plan. It might give me some time for a catch-up sleep."

Ten minutes later they were sitting down to her pancakes with maple syrup and vanilla ice cream, James chuckling at the retriever sitting close-by, his brown dog eyes beseeching and his mouth drooling.

"Here you go, Rocco," James said, throwing him a piece of the pancake without the syrup and ice cream. He chuckled as the dog caught it mid-air and wolfed it straight down.

"Rocco, you've had your breakfast," Marina scolded, but she couldn't help but giggle.

James sighed appreciation and scraped back his chair. "Your pancakes were delicious."

She bit into the last of her own pancake and nodded. "Thank you."

He stood. "Let me give you a hand with these dishes."

Marina found the task companionable, standing side-by-side at the sink, doing such a menial chore. James had his long sleeves rolled up past his elbows, his arms plunged into the soapy water. And Marina decided right then she could watch him like this for hours.

James Bowheart was a complicated man. And if she were a betting woman she'd wager his sixth sense often clashed with his razor sharp intellect and logic.

With the last dish on the drainer, he pulled the plug and let the water out. Turning to her, his expression serious, his soapy arms encircled her waist like it was the most natural action in the world. "Thank you," he murmured huskily.

"It was only breakfast," she managed to whisper.

"It was more than that," he said. "You've been there for me . . . for Josie, right from the start."

She couldn't drag her eyes away from his, and somehow they moved simultaneously, his head lowering while her head tilted back, her lips parting. When her belly collided against his burgeoning groin, they jerked apart like guilt-ridden, illicit lovers.

"I'm sorry," he rasped, lifting an arm then letting it fall to his side. "I totally misread—"

"No, you didn't. I wanted to kiss you, too." It'd felt so right having his mouth on hers. "I might be pregnant, but I'm not made of stone. I have feelings for you, too."

He took a step back, and she could see his inner conflict. She didn't blame him. How many young men wanted the responsibility of a soon-to-be, readymade family, let alone a man wrestling with the guilt of his mentally unstable sister?

"You should go have that sleep," she said softly. "I'll take Rocco for his walk. I'll be ready when you wake later."

James chugged down some water with his handful of pills, gripping the kitchen sink and closing his eyes to wait for some kind of solace to set in. But prerequisite self-loathing chased away much of the effects.

His thoughts drifted to Marina. She was way out of her depth if she thought he was any different than her ex-husband. She hated drug users. And though she might like him now, sooner or later she'd uncover the real him, and hate him for it.

If he was half the man she imagined him to be, he'd be cooling it off with her right now. He'd never committed to anyone before, and right then he seriously wondered if he would, could, ever live drug-free.

He'd be a fool not to try.

He opened his eyes on a sigh that was half weary resignation, half bliss. The effects of the pills were at last kicking in, and on shaky legs he made his way to his bedroom and flopped onto his bed.

He felt close to delirious with the sudden tiredness sweeping through his veins. How many pills had he swallowed? In some deep place inside his head an alarm rang, but overriding it was the sheer relief of drifting into the sweet, welcoming arms of oblivion . . .

He woke with a start, oddly disorientated. Yawning, he climbed out of bed, the walls looming and distorted. He shook his head and staggered from his bedroom, muttering, "Damn drugs."

The front door was open. He saw a person silhouetted in the afternoon haze. He stilled with a frown, scrunching his eyes. "Josie?"

She shook her head. Well, of course she was in denial. She was supposed to be in hospital, getting better.

She turned away and drifted gracefully down the steps.

James followed, calling out hoarsely, "Josie, wait!"

His voice induced some weird kind of reaction in his sister. She stopped, pointing at something he couldn't see. Staring fixatedly ahead, her arms began swinging rhythmically in time to her feet, and like a soldier marching to war she headed out of his front yard.

She turned right towards the main thoroughfare when a dog—Rocco—appeared seemingly from out of nowhere, trotting obediently by her side.

Marina would have already taken Rocco for a walk, he thought abstractedly. Besides, Josie wouldn't go near a dog that looked the image of Max.

Max? He shook his head. *Impossible.*

He strode after her faster, but suddenly his feet were leaden, heavy. "No!" he uttered, watching helplessly, frantically as Josie kept on marching down his street. She veered onto the main road, then she and the golden retriever moved quickly out of sight.

"Wait!" he croaked. It was imperative he follow her, his every instinct telling him not to lose sight.

A dog yelped. He heard a car horn, the squeal of brakes. Fear assaulted him, but suddenly he was exhausted, out of breath, and no longer able to put one foot in front of the other. He dropped to his knees, making it two houses down from his own on his neighbor's front lawn.

He fisted his hands, covering his eyes. "What is happening to me?" he groaned.

Was it the drugs? It had to be. He couldn't think beyond that possibility.

"Are you alright, mate?"

A stranger's deep voice had him look up sharply. A middle-aged, dark-skinned man with his brow damp with sweat, a fedora hat jammed onto his head, peered down at him with concern.

James managed a stiff nod. "I'm . . . fine."

Only, he wasn't fine. Not one bit. He was no longer anywhere near his house. In fact, there were no houses either side of the wide stretch of paved road.

The gates of a cemetery were across the road in front of him, and he lurched heavily to his feet when he caught a flash of silver-blond hair in the spill of late sunlight.

The other man reached out to steady him. James gasped out a breath, keeling over double as a lightning strike of pain shot through the middle of his chest. The stranger drew back and like a switch flicked off, the pain disappeared like it had never been.

James straightened ever so carefully, unable to drag his attention from the stranger.

The other man's face wore a look of bewilderment as he doffed his felt hat. Climbing onto an ancient pushbike that lay nearby, abandoned, he said, "I hope you find what you're looking for, my friend."

James answered with an abstracted nod, his legs functioning normally again as he headed across the road. He heard a dog bark once, twice. But as he stopped between the tall, white-railed gates, silence was all-encompassing.

He scanned right and left, his pulse thudding loud and erratic in his ears. Had he imagined seeing Josie? There was nothing here but endless rows of white headstones . . .

He stepped back with a shiver, goose-bumps crawling over his flesh. White headstones. Was this the graveyard he'd seen, no, hallucinated two days earlier in some wacked-out vision alone in Josie's hospital room?

It was. He was certain of it.

He backed away another couple of steps, and the seemingly invisible dog let loose with another low-pitched woof, echoing and eerie. And James couldn't shake the sudden feeling his every move was being monitored.

He had to get away from here.

He swung around, searching for the gracious stranger to ask for directions . . . ask for help.

There wasn't a soul in sight.

A bike bell pealed in the sudden gust of wind that sent leaves scudding and bouncing across the empty, narrow concrete pathway stretching far either side. Only, the sound hadn't come from outside the gates. It had come from within them.

A truth will be found at the cemetery ground.

James woke abruptly, Josie's words echoing in his head. He bolted upright, breathing heavily. His throat was dry and rasping. Sweat dribbled from his brow.

He glanced at his alarm clock. Two-forty-five p.m. He'd been asleep a little over five hours.

He jumped at the sudden joyful barking of a dog then sighed with relief. Rocco's barking had clearly intruded into his dreams. Climbing out of bed, he drew apart his bedroom window blinds and peered blearily through the gaps.

Marina was in her backyard, throwing a tennis ball for Rocco to chase down. The bangles on her wrists sounded like delicate chimes in a breeze . . . like the bell on a bike.

James smiled in relief, his tension easing further at the pure enjoyment of the scene. Marina was lovely in her bright yellow sundress, her baby bump visible beneath. A rainbow scarf tied her glorious hair back, a gold anklet chain glinting just above one of her canvas shoes.

Nudging the blind until it rolled up with a thwack, he slid open the window and called out, "Sorry I slept so long." When she turned and smiled warmly, waving up to him, his heart glowed. He cleared his throat. "Give me ten minutes."

After the world's quickest shower, he dressed into the most casual clothes he could find, jeans and a short-sleeved chambray shirt. Pulling on his footwear, he made his way into the kitchen to begin organizing the contents of a picnic basket.

*

"Watch your step," James warned. He held out a hand that wasn't already clamped to the picnic basket, guiding Marina over the rocky terrain that seemed little better than a goat track.

She stumbled. His grip tightened on her hand and he felt a frown furrow his brow. He hadn't remembered this path ever being so rough, so impractical for a heavily pregnant woman. Clearly he hadn't given this hike too much thought at all.

"Relax," Marina said with a wry grin. She hoisted the straps of her small backpack, which she'd insisted on carrying, into a more comfortable position across her shoulders. "I'm not made out of glass, you know."

James' frown eased as a smile formed of his own. There was something about this woman that made him happy, alive. "I know," he conceded. "But still, I don't want you to slip."

His hand stayed curled over hers as she stepped over the crumbling rock and came to stand before him. Even with the advantage of being on the elevated slope she had to tilt her head back to meet his gaze. Her beautiful eyes shone. "I know you'll keep me safe, James."

His heart wrenched with something too close to yearning. He didn't deserve even this fledgling of her faith. He managed a nod before clearing his too tight throat. "I'll do my best."

When he turned to lead the way, he didn't let her hand go. It felt right somehow to have their fingers interlaced as they traversed the last ten minutes of the downhill track to the basin of Green Moss Falls.

On private property, which he and only a few other people were allowed access, it was a secluded Garden of Eden.

They stood at a respectful distance from the waterfall, which streamed over a spectacular forty-meter drop off into a large pool surrounded by mossy boulders.

Just meters away tree ferns marched backward beneath the towering canopies of mountain ash, whose ribbons of white-gray bark dangled high up from their massive trunks.

"Wow, it's beautiful," Marina said. "I can't believe it's hidden away in here."

James' hand tightened once again as he watched her awestruck expression. The falls were spectacular, but for him it was little more than a backdrop to Marina's lovely profile.

She turned to him with sparkling eyes, about to say more. His face must have been an open book. Right away her lashes fluttered downward, her lips parting in surprise.

He brushed a thumb over her wrist, aware her pulse hammered in her veins. And even over the thunder of the falls he could hear her accelerated breaths, feel her anticipation, her tremor of anxiety.

"I'm sorry," he murmured. "I didn't mean to stare. Truth is, I wanted to kiss you. But I know you're not ready—"

His words were cut short as she went onto her tiptoes and covered his mouth with her own. Her lips were soft, satiny, and almost voluptuous on his, and he stayed frozen in shocked disbelief and growing arousal.

She eased back, so very assured. "Don't be sorry," she whispered. She drew in a deep breath. "I know we haven't spent a whole lot of time together, but I've learned to trust my instincts, even with my reservations." She expelled a gentle sigh. "I . . . I think I'm falling for you, James."

He couldn't speak. Not yet. His throat was all but clogged with emotion. That Marina trusted him enough to have such feelings for him, let alone to admit it, words couldn't explain how much it meant to him.

"You're falling for another addict," he said softly. "I don't want that." Her eyes clouded. He tilted her chin, holding her stare. "If there is any chance for us . . . I have to quit."

"You'd do that for me?"

"I would." He nodded even while he gritted his teeth against the sudden surge of need—far different from the one in his loins.

He dropped his hand and averted his gaze, lowering the picnic basket onto the ground.

She might like him now, but she most certainly wouldn't if he ever gave into the temptation of his habit, ever went back on his word. Swallowing the bitter pill of his own weakness, he reached inside the basket and withdrew a rolled-up blanket.

Marina swept a hand towards the overhang of a craggy rock, thankfully changing the topic of conversation. "There's shade over there."

He spread the blanket out onto the sandy, relatively flat ground, where ferns edged a sharp embankment skirting the pool of clear, green-tinged water.

Marina slipped off her backpack and put it down, then sat on the blanket with a relieved little sigh. James pushed aside self-doubts and worried again if she'd overexerted herself. Although it was late afternoon, it was still unseasonably hot.

"Are you alright?" He kneeled beside her, anxiety pressing at his sensibilities as he noted her flushed face.

"I'm fine, James." She smiled up at him. "Truly."

He suppressed the niggling doubts that had bothered him all afternoon. Of course she'd be fine. Reaching forward, he brushed a lock of satiny gold hair from her face. "Sorry, I guess I'm over-reacting," he murmured huskily. "I just want you to be safe."

"Thank you." Marina was gravely serious. "Aside from my parents, no one's ever really protected me before." She nodded, her face flushing an even deeper pink. "It's nice."

He stood and turned away, oddly flustered himself as he retrieved the picnic basket. Sitting beside her, he pulled out two plastic champagne flutes. Handing her one, he freed the champagne bottle from a foil sleeve that kept it cool. Lifting the bottle with a flourish, he revealed the label. "Non-alcoholic."

Marina's eyes twinkled, her lips curving into a smile. "You've really thought of everything."

He couldn't draw in breath as he wondered for a few crazy seconds what she'd do if he leaned over and kissed her this time. Only, did he want to stop at just kissing? Need for her had been a constant, internal simmer from the moment he'd seen her standing beside her driveway.

Her kiss—that kiss—just moments ago had warmed his blood. There was no doubt he was attracted to her physically, but what about emotionally? Did he trust these feelings coming to life deep inside?

He'd never before considered a serious relationship, never gone beyond the short term with a woman. Why would he? He'd seen the wreckage that was his parents' marriage.

Distracting his thoughts from a path he no longer wanted to travel, he fished out a corkscrew and set about the tedious process of uncorking the bottle. It popped, and somehow the tension between them evaporated right along with it.

He grinned. And even before the foamy bubbles had cascaded from its top he was filling their glasses. He raised his glass in a toast. "To health and happiness."

She smiled, her eyes holding his as she added, "To us."

The non-alcoholic liquid didn't dislodge the sudden lump in his throat as he gulped it down, nor did it slow the erratic beat of his heart.

Marina put down her drink, serious suddenly. "I visited Josie yesterday, on my own, after we'd seen her."

"You did?"

"Yes." She chewed her lower lip. "I felt so bad about her book, I wanted to make it up to her somehow."

"She's not your responsibility."

"No. But she's my friend. I want her to be happy."

Could there be a more beautiful person? Right then James doubted it very much. "I'm afraid the only person to make Josie happy, is Josie."

"Perhaps. But having a friend, someone she can trust, is important."

James put a hand over hers. "You're right. I'm sure Josie values your friendship."

Marina's eyes softened. "Not as much as she values her big brother's love."

He raised a brow. "Sometimes I wonder about that."

She turned her hand in his, clasping his fingers and giving a squeeze. "I don't." Releasing hold, she dragged her backpack closer before rummaging inside and carefully withdrawing Josie's poetry book.

James felt his belly tighten just by the sight of his sister's book. Suddenly it seemed all too probable his gift to her was to blame for all the eerie happenings in his life of late. "What is that doing here?" he muttered.

Marina glanced up from where she was flicking through the pages. "There's a page Josie has marked that I thought might interest you."

This is just a quick note, bro, written on tissues—they're all I could find

A tangle of sentences torn from my mind and scrawled, barely scratching the surface,

I'm so god dammed nervous of showing my feelings to you.

This is just a quick note, bro—I'm struggling here, pencil dragging the tissue—

I need to write this to say how I'll miss you.

Do you really have to go?

This is just a quick note to thank you, bro, for fighting my fights, standing up for my rights,

Sticking with me though I never thanked you then, you'd just do it again—me with my big mouth

Getting in strife; on one occasion, you saved my life, saved me from some sordid knife that was thrust at me instead of fists—

Mate, I could never list the times you've helped me out . . .

So what's this all about?

Do you really have to go, bro?"

~Sue Allen

Marina stopped reading. "That's so deep, James. She really cares about you."

He nodded, moved by the words Marina had read. His sister might not have written the poem, but she'd marked it, had probably read it over and over.

The beautiful notes of a bellbird abruptly rang out.

Marina snapped shut the book and tucked it carefully into her backpack, breaking the intimate moment. "It's so hot. Let's go for a swim."

James nodded, only too glad for the diversion. Josie didn't have to feature in his thoughts, his mind, twenty-four-seven. With a grin, he gestured at his clothes and said, "Only if you don't mind seeing me in my underwear."

Marina unbuttoned her pants and stepped out of them. "Only if you don't mind seeing me in mine." She giggled at his apparently shell-shocked expression, and then pulled up her T-shirt to stand before him in knickers and bra, her belly a lovely bump.

Damn, she was beautiful.

"Last one in is a rotten egg!" she dared.

Before he'd even scrambled onto his feet to drag off his clothes, she was slipping over the edge and into the water, turning onto her back so that her belly was protruding and glistening in the setting sun.

She laughed and kicked away from the bank as he stripped down to his boxer briefs. He dived in after her, the sudden hit of the water around him bitingly cold. Staying underwater, he swam in the direction she'd headed, seeing the phosphorous bubbles churned by her impressively strong kicks.

He broke the surface beside her, and she let out a little shriek, splashing his face reflexively with an open palm.

"Oh, James, I'm sorry. It's just . . . you scared me!"

Treading water, he put his hands up momentarily in mock surrender. "Hey, don't apologize! I'll just remember next time not to sneak up on you."

"Are you saying there's going to be a next time?" she asked, her smile belying the seriousness lurking in her stare.

No! "Yes." His voice came out husky as he pushed some wet hair from her face. "I can't stop thinking about you. Even with my eyes closed, I see your face."

Her stare turned soft, almost needy. "I haven't been able to stop thinking about you, either." Then her arms were sliding behind his neck, her fingers in his hair and her legs around his waist. As their lips met he forgot to breathe, forgot to kick.

Desire roared through his veins as they sank underwater, mouths still merged. Only when breathing became imperative did they part and then swim to shore, clambering onto the blanket before moving into each other's arms and continuing their kiss.

James pulled back, aware just how close he really was to taking her here. And as Marina pressed kisses to his brow, his nose, his throat, he said, "I want you, so badly. But I'm not sure it's a good idea. For you or the baby."

She lifted her stare to his. "Have you ever been told you think too much sometimes?" She cupped his face, her dreamy expression fading only slightly as she said, "James. I thank you for your concern, I really do. But I'm a responsible adult, okay?"

He stayed silent, conflicted, and so very, very aroused. "I've been with many, many women," he admitted. "But sex with them was meaningless. It won't be with you."

She nodded, her face flushed.

"What I feel for you goes beyond sex, is way deeper than anything I've experienced before," he said.

"Thank you."

He kissed her again, taking his time, savoring her delectable mouth. When he drew her close by cupping her nape with its wild tangle of wet hair, he broke the kiss to murmur, "You're still wet. I don't want you getting cold."

"You'll keep me warm, James." She pulled back, and, lifting her arms behind her, unclipped her bra. Her beautiful breasts spilled free, tipped with rosy nipples that he immediately imagined taking into his mouth.

She slowly pulled down her panties. The last rays of sunlight gilded her hair, caressing her soft skin.

"Are you testing me?" he rasped thickly. "I'm no saint."

"I know." She smiled almost demurely, and James truly wondered if any angel could be half as beautiful. "But I trust you, James. Trust that if things go further, you'll take care of me."

Even with the rapidly cooling afternoon air, his arousal strained within the confines of his damp boxer briefs. She kneeled beside him, helping him divest his last piece of clothing. Her hands so close to his groin caused his breath to noisily exhale, his erection to jump when her knuckles brushed his inner thighs.

Kissing again, almost instinctively they moved in synch onto their knees, mouths separating momentarily until they were lying down and facing each other. James draped the blanket across their bared skin, cocooning them as they pressed together, intimate yet not joined.

Marina broke the kiss with a little sigh, her eyes bright in the night looming around them. "I've only ever been with one man."

His chest hurt. "Your husband was a lucky man."

"Thank you." But the sudden downcast tilt of her face told him her fool of a husband had thought otherwise.

With the waterfall serenading them, he tilted her chin, bringing her beautiful, glistening eyes back to meet his stare. "When we make love, I promise you it will be extra special," he said huskily.

"I believe you," she whispered, so very serious it caused his heart to ache.

Her breasts brushed his chest. His breath came out in a hiss, his groin clenching when she lifted a thigh and rested it on top of his.

She was pushing all the right buttons, but no matter how much he wanted to, he wouldn't take her. He'd made a promise to abstain from drugs, and until he was completely drug-free, he'd abstain from making love to her, too.

Their first time together really would be perfect.

He kissed her quivering lips and she sighed against his mouth. "I'm not sure I can wait," she admitted.

Desperation rang in his sudden bark of laughter. She giggled, acknowledging what he felt, what she felt. And suddenly they were both laughing hard, gasping for breath, shattering their almost exquisite yearning.

James couldn't place the moment they fell asleep. He remembered their laughter subsiding, remembered them kissing in-between murmuring inconsequential stuff, cuddling.

Next thing he knew, he was wide-awake. Dawn had broken. And he lay in a warm, wet puddle.

Marina's eyes were wide in a face that had leached of all color. "James, I think my water broke."

Chapter Four

Green Moss Falls, Australia
Tuesday, March 15th

"I sure hope you know how to deliver a baby in the middle of nowhere—" Marina gasped as another contraction hit. "—if we don't make it to hospital in time.

"I said I'd look after you," James said.

When she stilled beside him, her breaths coming fast and urgent, he adjusted her backpack across his shoulders and bent down, sweeping her up into his arms. Pressing a kiss to the crown of her head, he added, "And I meant it."

Shell-shocked with pain, her contractions just minutes apart, she only made token resistance when he carried her between the cramps, setting her back onto her feet so she could lean against him as the next contraction hit.

Damn it, she was early. But at thirty-six weeks, not too early, surely? The chances of fetal problems should be minimal.

But he wasn't taking any chances!

He'd left his cell phone in his car, and after settling Marina into the passenger seat he made a brief, concise call to the professor, ensuring he'd meet them at the hospital and take charge of the delivery.

The professor agreed, and James disconnected before firing up the BMW's engine. The wheels kicked up stones behind them as he urged the car forward, back down the winding, pot-holed road as fast as he dared.

The hospital appeared practically deserted when they arrived just over an hour later. Marina was panting as she rode out the contractions, but stoically silent otherwise, putting all her energy into the labor.

A nurse brought out a wheelchair and as Marina was wheeled in the direction of the birthing suite, she yelled, "James!"

His pace quickening, he moved to her side.

Marina's eyes were a little wild when she said, "Don't leave me."

"I'm not going anywhere."

The professor was already gowned-up and ready to go. And this once James was relieved to simply go along for the ride, glad just to hold Marina's hand and be there for her.

A midwife checked the baby's heartbeat, and minutes later the professor confirmed what Marina instinctively knew. It was time to push.

An odd, euphoric calm settled over James as he watched Marina bear down, watched the miracle of giving birth unfold before him. An extraordinary revelation as old as time itself.

Never before had he experienced such a beautiful moment.

Though the pain was clearly intense, Marina was focused and determined.

The professor gave her a nod, then exclaimed, "The baby's crowning! It won't be long now and you'll be holding it in your arms." All doctor now, he focused on Marina and instructed, "Next push, bear down with everything you have."

The baby boy arrived at eight-fifty-two a.m. with a wail of good health.

Marina gave him a tired, but exhilarated smile. "James, will you cut the cord?"

He nodded, his breath catching in his throat. "It would be my honor."

There was something spiritual, something bonding about severing the umbilical cord from the baby's mother and never more so when he already shared such a deep connection with Marina.

When the midwife placed the red, wrinkled baby into Marina's arms, Marina whispered in awe, "Isn't he beautiful?"

"Just like his mother."

James bent down and kissed her brow, feeling odd inside, his chest aching and overflowing with tenderness.

When he left the hospital some three hours later—with Marina's house key and instructions where to find her hospital bag—his mind . . . his heart, was still trying to deal with the implications of his feelings.

The car beeped as James activated the keyless entry. Minutes later he was swinging out of the car park and heading towards the main arterial, a Cheshire grin splitting his face.

Had he ever felt this happy?

No drug in the world could compare to this!

He wanted to celebrate, to rejoice in the news of Marina giving birth.

Josie would be so excited.

He was scarcely aware of the tears streaming down his face until the green sedan in front blurred like mist and his BMW almost sailed into its rear end.

He took a deep, calming breath. He had to be more careful. He had so much to live for now.

On arrival at Karlcodi, he was directed to the common room. Coming to a standstill in the doorway, he found Josie with Matt and two other patients, but his sister sat alone, her face drawn.

Vivaldi played in the background. The beautiful notes were at odds to the female patient muttering to herself at one end of the table, obsessively twisting a Styrofoam cup, her lifeless male companion who sat opposite staring at a smear on the wall.

His smile faltered. Josie didn't belong here.

Matt was hunched over his tarot cards, almost as though he was hiding or protecting them, his orange-painted fingernails bright against his glittery, purple kimono.

James frowned. If he were on duty here, he'd discourage this kind of behavior. It seemed Tess didn't have a problem with it, but clearly other nurses did by how protective Matt was with the tarot cards.

Matt turned over a card, and James caught a glimpse of welt-like scars on his wrists before an image on the face of the card distracted him. A hangman? Matt quickly flipped the card back, his shoulders slumped, his breath wheezing.

James frowned, his mind clicking over. But his train of thought was disrupted when Josie cried, "No, Matt. Please, put them away."

He rushed forward. "Josie. Are you alright?"

In his peripheral, he saw Matt jerk out of his daze, all his attention turning to Josie before he did as she asked and pushed his tarot cards together, wrapping them carefully into a bright magenta silk scarf.

Josie gasped in a breath, visibly relaxing the hand at her throat as she turned to James and said, "I'm fine. At least, I am now. Sorry, I didn't mean to frighten you."

Typical of his sister, he thought. He'd taken away her poetry book, a thing she loved, and she worried more about his getting a fright than she did about her own health.

He drew her into his arms. She stiffened, but selfish as it was he needed the contact as much as she did.

She gradually relaxed again. Voice muffled, she said, "What is it, James?"

Did nothing escape her? "Marina had her baby this morning," he said thickly, his throat clogging with emotion.

Josie pulled back, her scare all but forgotten with her blue eyes sparkling like summer rain. "She did?" she squealed. She chewed her bottom lip, contemplative. "A boy," she mused aloud. "She had a boy."

He guessed the odds were good she'd know, either way. "Yes."

"I wish Molly was here to see him," she said abruptly, almost mournfully. "I miss her."

James frowned. Molly may have been a part of Josie's life, a part of Josie, for as long as he could remember, but why did she have to spoil the joyful moment and mention her absence now? "Maybe she's not coming back?" he suggested.

Her features flattened, hardened. "Don't say that, don't you dare say that!" she hissed.

"Jo-Josie. Is every th-thing okay?"

James turned to face Matt.

"Yes, I guess so," she said on a sigh.

Matt swung away. "Alright th-th-then."

James didn't want him to withdraw into his shell, not just yet. Too many questions remained unanswered. Only, as he put a hand on his shoulder, Matt abruptly shrank from his touch.

The other man's hysteria rose from his body quicker than the screams of terror that came out in a gabble of disjointed words.

Josie gagged suddenly, and James called out for a nurse as he went straight into doctor mode for his sister.

Her airway was clear, her throat unobstructed. But her pupils were dilated, her pulse rapid. All signs that led him to believe it was psychological trauma, not physical.

With a hysterical Matt coaxed out of the common room by two nurses, James noted how quickly Josie had returned to normal. Well, to herself.

"Does Matt do this to you?" he asked.

Josie gave a stiff nod. "I think so. Sometimes he makes my throat go funny."

Shit. She sounded like a little girl.

"You're going to have to stop seeing him. And why on earth is he allowed those cards anyway?" He was on a roll, sounding just like their Bowheart father and unable to stop. "Being subjected to them is not good for your recovery. I'm going to have to talk to someone about it."

"James. No. I . . . I know he hurts me, but it's not his fault. He's my only friend in here. The only one in the world who believes in Molly." She shook her head. "Surely you've felt what I have? Felt someone else's pain?" Tears welled. "Matt has been hurt, that's all."

James stared. This time the air left his lungs as he all but crumpled into the plastic chair at the table recently vacated by Matt.

"James." His sister had moved to stand beside him. And this time she looked down at him with the stare of someone worldly-wise and much, much older. Only her stare held the compassion and deep feeling that only one as kind and as caring as his sister could possibly express. "You've felt it, too, haven't you?"

Not unlike the specter they'd both seen in her room.

He sighed, raking both hands over his face. "I don't know, Josie, I really don't know."

The muttering of the other female patient jerked James out of his reverie. He stood. "Look at the time. I'd better go. I've got rounds to do in just over an hour and have to shower yet and grab Marina's bag for her."

Josie nodded, even while she wrung her hands. "James. Please, be careful driving."

His stomach lurched, almost as if reading her energy, but he buried the memory of his sister's hallucinogenic words. *James won't die. He won't!* "I'll be careful," he promised.

It was only when he walked down Karlcodi's corridor and he caught sight of a lone tarot card lying face-up on the floor and he bent to retrieve it that his stomach really heaved.

The black-robed skeleton with his scythe screamed death, even before he read that exact word on the bottom of the card.

Tess was at her usual station when he placed the tarot—facedown—in front of her. At her curious expression, he shrugged. "Sorry. I found it in the corridor. Matt's, I assume."

Tess turned it over, arching a ginger brow. "No doubt," she answered thoughtfully. "I'll be sure he gets it—"

"Do you think it's ethical to allow the patients this kind of freedom?" he asked, once again feeling every inch like his overbearing father but too unnerved by Josie's earlier reaction to care. "My sister gets upset with his readings, and I'm sure plenty of other patients would to."

Tess looked back at the lone card. "Perhaps you're right. Perhaps I've been too lenient by turning a blind eye."

James felt the tension leave his body. "I'm only glad you're being reasonable."

Tess straightened up some paperwork on her desk. "Yes, well, I'm not cut from the same arrogant cloth of some of the staff around here."

Doctor Leonard.

The name filled his head as though the word had been spoken aloud. Only, it hadn't. He cleared his throat, dismissing the notion. "I'm glad."

Tess nodded in response. Brightening suddenly, she said, "By the way, how is Marina?" Giving a conspiratorial wink, she added, "She visited the night before, you know."

James felt a huge grin form, all the bad stuff again evaporating. "Marina has never been better. She had a baby boy just a little while ago."

Tess clapped her hands together. "How wonderful! Congratulations."

James was still grinning half an hour later as he showered and then dressed for his rounds at work. Going next door, he gave Rocco a quick pat and his morning feed, before he snaffled the pre-packed bag from Marina's sunshine-yellow bedroom, and all but jogged to his car.

If he was quick, he'd get to spend a couple of minutes with Marina and the baby before starting his rounds. And tomorrow he'd buy her the biggest, brightest bunch of flowers he could find.

At the hospital, he pushed through the double doors of the maternity ward. Minutes later he was directed to her room, where he found Marina propped up on some pillows, the bed slightly elevated.

Her baby lay in her arms beside her, sound asleep and swaddled in a little blue blanket.

A picture of angelic innocence.

"James," she murmured throatily. As he placed her bag beside her bed she smiled. "Thanks."

"You're welcome." He placed the backpack she'd lugged to Green Moss Falls, which he'd taken out of his car at the last minute, beside her hospital bag. "I thought you might like this, too."

"You're so thoughtful."

He'd been called many things in his life, but thoughtful wasn't one of them. "How are you feeling?"

"Totally awestruck by the fact I have a baby."

"You'll make a fine mother," he said huskily.

Her eyes sparkled up at him. "I hope so."

The baby snuffled then, his tiny hands fisting and his pink lips pursing before he abruptly yawned.

Marina scooped him up. "Would you like to hold him?"

James felt suddenly inadequate as she handed her precious bundle to him. But as he looked down at the little guy, held his tiny weight, something powerful clicked inside him . . . a connection that transcended even the biological.

"I decided to call him Alexander James," she said softly, proudly.

He dragged his gaze away from her baby. "I love it." *I love you.* "But are you sure about James, I mean?"

"Never more sure of anything in my life," she said softly. "You're forever connected to us now."

His heart swelled, primitive and almost possessive emotions filling him to the brim until he was overflowing with pride, with joy. With love. "Thank you."

She lifted a hand and placed it on his thigh, an intimate gesture of propriety that felt so damn right. "No, thank you," she said softly.

He sat beside her on the hospital bed, and her hand stayed right where it was on his thigh, her fingertips gently stroking.

She sat forward. "What you said earlier, about kicking the habit." At his nod, she continued. "If you succeed, I'd really like to see you more." She glanced at Alexander in his arms, her eyes shining with love. "We'd like to see you more."

He nodded. What better cause for motivation could there possibly be? "I'd like that, too."

Leaning over carefully and reaching for the backpack on the floor, she pulled out Josie's poetry book. "Do you think you should return this to your sister?" Marina asked gently.

James smiled. "I guess I probably should."

She flipped open the book, turning its pages reverently, the tip of her tongue wedged between her teeth. "There is one poem in here I'd like to read. It's just so perfect for us right now." She nodded. "Ah, here it is."

Your sweet eyes, dark as night they waver, resting on my face.
Tiny baby breaths exhaled, perfume my breathing space.
Your hand unfurls and wrinkled fingers clasp my hair;
Of what it is they grasp, or why I gasp—still unaware . . .
Your tiny calves; soft boomerangs of pliant bone, slip into fetal form,
The shape in which you nestled long before your soul was born.
Nine months you shared my resting place, pressed for space—
I felt your vibrant push and thrust, the heady rush of flickers in my core—
You heard my body's roar . . .
A rushing ocean pumping by, crimson as an evening sky,
And perhaps you heard your mother sigh as drifting off to sleep,
My heartbeat thudded slow and deep . . .
I hold you cradled in my arms, beguiled by all your baby charms
I picture you a man full grown, and flown into a life anew!
So sacred are these moments with you resting on my knee—
Me simply loving you and you simply loving me . . .
You'll never be alone in existence on this Earth,
Joy and love will follow you from this, your day of birth,
A life alive with happiness encapsulating mirth;

Carefree as a boat upon the sea!
My love for you, shall everlasting be . . ."
~Sue Allen

Alexander let out a sudden wail, his tiny pink face screwed up into a deep frown.

"He must be hungry," Marina said, setting the poetry book close to James before undoing the laces on the back of her hospital gown. "It will be nice to get back into my own clothes again," she said with a husky chuckle.

James reluctantly handed Alexander back to his mother and Marina smiled at her son, cooing softly to calm him until he latched onto her exposed breast and fed.

"He's already going to sleep," she whispered tenderly.

James watched, his heart aching at the picture. So surreal. So peaceful. Taking hold of the poetry book, he leaned forward, catching Marina's mouth with his for a short, but meaningful kiss. "I have to get going," he said. "But I'll see you again tonight, okay?"

"Okay, James," she said quietly, her eyes brimming. "Thank you for everything."

He was fifteen minutes late by the time he exited the elevator on the second floor and caught up with Doc Moore and the small group of medical students who were doing general practice rounds.

At his approach, a sneer reserved exclusively for James settled over the doctor's face. "Ah, how kind of you to join us."

James nodded, choosing silence as the better option. He wasn't about to make apologies to a man who'd exaggerate and gloat over any acknowledgement of wrongness.

The doctor continued to drone on to his assembled students, explaining his diagnosis in a step-by-excruciating-step process. Clearly James had missed the part where the student doctors were given a chance to diagnose the patient first.

Tom raised a brow as James joined them, and gave him a conspiratorial wink. Leaning forward, Tom murmured, "Doc Bore got out of the wrong side of bed this morning."

Doc Moore jerked his head up, setting his sights on the two of them. "Tom, I take it you were bringing James up to speed on our next patient?"

After a little round of snickers, Doc Moore's eyes narrowed contemplatively. "James, perhaps you would like to give your diagnosis first?"

James shrugged, a gesture that he knew infuriated the good doctor. "Sure." Thrusting Josie's poetry book under an arm, he flicked through the notes on the chart at the end of the bed.

Pulse of sixty-nine beats per minute. Blood pressure equal at both arms of around one hundred and fifteen over seventy. Slightly tachypnoeic and diaphoretic. Ear, nose, and throat examination did not provide any diagnostic clues as to the cause of the pharyngeal pain.

Doc Moore moved to draw him alongside the patient. "Here we have Baxter Purcell." He gave a nod to the man lying in the bed before continuing his spiel. "Blood samples have been taken and sent to lab. I've arranged a CT scan for this afternoon. Diagnosis has yet to be confirmed, though we suspect—"

James was aware Doc Moore continued his prognosis, but his voice had become background noise to the disorientating sense of déjà-vu that overcame him, leaving him speechless the moment he locked eyes with the dark-skinned patient.

Baxter's breath came short and fast as he rasped, "You look like you've seen a ghost," a thread of impatience somehow audible in every note.

James mentally pulled himself out of his state-of-shock. "Sorry . . . have we . . . met before?"

Tom murmured beside him, "Nice pick-up line," to another round of snickers from those who could hear.

Doc Moore's scowl deepened. "Well, James," he prompted. "What is your professional opinion?"

Baxter frowned at the group gathered around his bed, his stare resting on James. "If you've come to jab yet another needle into my tired old veins, forget it."

Putting a brake on the chaotic thoughts whirling around his head a million miles an hour, James reassured, "No, Baxter, ah, Mr. Purcell, I'm not here to take more of your blood." He tried an encouraging smile. "How about we start from the very beginning to how you're feeling right now?"

Baxter clamped a hand to his neck. "I just want someone to fix my throat. The pain's agonizing, like nothing I've ever had before. The stabbing sensation started this morning and hasn't let up. Even a shot of morphine the nurse gave me earlier hasn't helped."

"So on a scale of one to ten, what is your pain level at now?"

Baxter's fingers massaged gently up and down his neck. "If ten is dead, I'm sitting close to a nine."

"Okay. What about in general terms?"

"How should I know, Doc? I just feel . . . wrung out. Like overcooked porridge. Old, lumpy, and vile." Baxter swept out a hand. "Speaking of which, the folks at Meals on Wheels will be wondering—" He sucked in a fitful breath. "—where I am. I cook a mean stew for those who appreciate a little hot food in their belly."

James swallowed a lump in his throat. He should have known this man wasn't impatient without good reason. He didn't want to be helped; he wanted to help others. "Well, hopefully we'll have you back on your feet and cooking soon."

Baxter gave an almost imperceptible nod. "I'll hold you to that."

"Mind if I take your pulse?" James asked.

Baxter turned his wrist so that his pulse was within easy access. "Sure," he said, resigned.

James placed the clipboard and poetry book onto the bedside before pressing two fingers against Baxter's pulse. A surge of heat, undiluted and red-raw, sent him staggering backwards.

Josie's poetry book crashed to the floor and the clipboard flipped over and over, before it, too, clattered onto the floor.

James sucked in a breath, holding in the pain until he felt it slowly recede, then disappear. Murmuring an apology, he crouched to retrieve the clipboard and book from off the floor.

Get a grip. Don't lose it now. Not here.

His eyes narrowed. In big bold letters and underlined, the words AORTIC ANEURISM were noted on the chart. Of course, the clinical chameleon!

Sweeping up the chart, it wasn't until he retrieved Josie's poetry book from where it lay on Baxter's overnight bag that he spied the fedora hat on the floor nearby . . . the very same hat he'd seen in his vision.

A sudden bout of dizziness assailed him, his mind all but shutting down. He gripped the side of Baxter's bed, nausea filling his belly. What was happening to him? What did it all mean?

Baxter frowned. "Is there a problem?"

"No . . . no. I agree with what's on the chart," James mumbled, all but thrusting it to Doc Moore. As the other doctor flipped through the notes, a frown on his face, James said, "Aortic dissection."

Doc Moore raised a brow. "Aortic dissection?" He passed the chart to Tom. "Anyone else agree with James?"

Tom frowned, staring at James with a skeptical gleam. "Ah, James, there's nothing here that mentions AA. And with these symptoms it would be unlikely."

Doc Moore shook his head, smoothing things over with the patient. "Please excuse our young James, he's under a bit of pressure lately." He turned to James. "I think maybe you should take the rest of the day off."

James bit back a retort. Instead, he gripped Josie's poetry book to his chest and gave a nod. "Perhaps you're right," he clipped out before turning on his heel and pushing through the small crowd of student doctors.

Tom caught up to him as he strode out of the room. "Hey, what happened back there?" he asked. "What have you been taking?"

James stilled beside his friend. "I'm not taking anything. I've been clean for days. But for once Doc Moore is right. I'm taking a few days off."

Tom snorted out a laugh, clapping him on the shoulder. "So that's your problem! Withdrawal isn't fun, my man, but easily fixed." With a cocky grin, he murmured, "Go see Stevie in Ward Five. She'll get you sorted. I'll give her a call."

For a moment, temptation left his mind whirling with need. Then, "No, I'm not going back to where I was."

Tom shook his head. "Look at yourself! You're a mess, my friend. Your career and credibility is on the line." He stepped back. "Stevie will be expecting you."

James stepped into the elevator and pressed the button to the maternity ward. Clutching Josie's book to his chest, he turned to Tom. "Tell her not to bother."

A few minutes later when he entered Marina's room, she greeted him with a wide smile. "How lovely to see you. I wasn't expecting you back so soon!"

"Just try keeping me away," he said, managing a smile in return and feeling every one of his anxieties melt away.

She glowed with pride. "I'm about to give Alexander his first bath. Want to help?"

He stepped forward. "Please."

Minutes later, Marina was supporting Alexander's head, keeping his face well out of the water in the portable baby bath, while James drizzled warm water over the baby's little belly.

"He loves the water," Marina murmured, maternal pride filling her every word. "He's going to sleep."

"I guess he thinks he's back in your womb."

Marina nodded. "You're probably right."

After drying Alexander carefully, dressing him and wrapping him snug in his blanket, Marina tucked him into his crib and motioned for James to sit on the bed beside her.

"Something is on your mind. Do you want to talk about it?"

James sat near her, shaking his head with ironic humor. "You know me so well already?"

"I guess I do."

He lifted a hand and then let it drop back to his side.

"Something happened the other day . . . something kind of . . . weird."

She took hold of his hand. "Your kind of weird is my kind of normal, James."

He turned to her, feeling the love for her swell out of his chest and beam from his eyes. "That's one of the things I adore about you," he whispered.

He leaned forward and she leaned forward. Their lips met on a breathless sigh. His hands moved up and cupped her face, and using his fingertips he explored her expression, felt her emotions like a blind man reading Braille.

She appeared to be half-dazed when they pulled apart. He knew exactly how she felt. Somehow Marina made him forget everything but the good stuff.

"So . . . what happened?" she said.

He ran the back of his knuckles across her soft, just-kissed lips. "I dreamed about Josie and her dog. I tried to follow them when they left the yard." He grimaced. "Suddenly I was in front of a graveyard. A man I never met asked me if I was okay."

When he paused, she said, "Go on."

"I'd never met him before in my life. But just before I come here, I saw him in the hospital, in bed. I think he's dying."

Chapter Five

Carlton, Australia

Wednesday, March 16th

The early morning sky was a cloudless canvas of sapphire blue, the air crisp, clean, and invigorating without the usual city smog.

James pushed himself to run faster, his long strides eating up the ground. Damn, he'd forgotten how good it felt to press himself physically, to have his heart thud, his lungs cry for oxygen, his skin damp with sweat and his leg muscles burning.

To be drug-free.

He needed to keep moving, keep his mind occupied as much as he needed to sweat the chemicals out of his system.

Tom was right. His body was even now going through withdrawals. He'd known it from the moment he'd climbed into bed last night and experienced the first signs of cramps and cold sweats. He'd craved something, anything, like never before. A single aspirin would have sufficed.

But knowing Marina and Alexander were waiting for him at the top of his personal Everest kept him strong. As tough and rocky as his climb might be, it was a journey that had to be done.

Coming to a crossroads where the traffic zoomed past thick and fast, he drew to a stop. Hands on his knees, he stayed motionless a few minutes as he regained his breath.

A familiar-sounding bike bell tinkled on the footpath behind him, the swish of its tires moving around him.

Baxter?

Impossible.

He stared in disbelief.

The dark-skinned man flickered in and out of focus like an old movie reel that wasn't quite working. His ancient bike dropped to the ground with a clatter. Everything distorted again, and then stabilized for a couple of seconds. Baxter clutched his chest, his face ashen as he looked up at James and pleaded, "Help me, please. Hurry."

The image dissolved like mist, and without thought, James wheeled around and ran. He was only a few blocks away from home.

An old lady hosing the leaves on her pathway looked up when her fluffy white dog raced along the front fence, yapping and barely keeping pace with James. He was turning into his own yard by the time the elderly woman called her dog back.

A minute later, still in his sweats and joggers, James was pulling out onto the main arterial and heading towards Princeton Private.

Green traffic lights ahead blinked to amber and then red. He braked to a stop, checking his watch. *Damn it!* He had to hurry.

A truck pulled to a stop beside him, its loud hiss of air brakes spiking his adrenaline before dragging him back to reality.

Who was he trying to kid? He was practically a qualified doctor. What was he doing running off to the hospital in jogging sweats to check up on a patient he'd seen in a what? A vision? A dream? An hallucination?

He'd blamed popping pills for giving him visions, but it was obvious coming off those same drugs made the hallucinations even worse.

A lady in an overly tight cream business skirt and jacket strutted across the pedestrian crossing in her high heels. A young couple clad in blue jeans and 'Save the Planet' T-shirts strolled behind her, arm-in-arm, only half aware of the world around them.

So normal. So predictable.

Everything his life wasn't.

His gaze moved to the passenger seat, to Josie's poetry book. Guilt stirred to life. The sooner he gave the book back to his sister, the better. He should never have taken it away from her in the first place. Sometimes his own arrogance astounded even him.

The lights turned green. The truck roared to life beside him and moved forward. A horn sounded behind him. Then another. Taking a deep, calming breath, James put his car into gear. The BMW leapt forward.

Hallucination or not, there was no harm in easing his mind.

After parking his car, he strode through the hospital's entrance doors. Minutes later, he exited the elevator on the second floor. A nurse, her expression somber, ushered two patients down the corridor, the wheels on their IV poles squeaking in protest.

Baxter's roommates?

Pulse hammering, he broke into a run. He slammed to a stop in the doorway, confronted by a hive of frantic activity.

Nurses were working around Baxter like a well-oiled machine. One pushed a resuscitation trolley into place, another quickly and efficiently cleared the bedside area while yet another gave Baxter sedation drugs via a cannula.

Doc Moore was busy inserting a tube down Baxter's throat, and James immediately scanned the heart monitor machine. Baxter was bradycardic, his blood pressure dropping fast. He peered harder, frowning. On closer inspection, he realized the patient was in a junctional rhythm.

Doc Moore looked up then. He motioned to a nurse to shut the curtain, and it closed around them with a metallic *thwitt.*

James fisted his hands, his head pounding. Whether in anger or in need of a fix, he wasn't sure. He focused on what he could hear, only too aware of the procedures involved.

Doc Moore's authoritative voice barked out orders to the nurses. "Ring ahead and advise to prep for an urgent CT scan. Patient is flat and we don't know what's wrong. And cross match three units of blood."

A nurse pushed past James as she hurried out of the room to do Doc Moore's bidding.

James swiped a hand over his face. No. No. No. No! He had a bad feeling about this, a gut instinct that there was no more time to lose. When the nurses wheeled Baxter out of the room, Doc Moore in the lead, James said, "I think he needs to go straight to theater. A type A aortic dissection needs a surgeon and anesthetist."

Doc Moore didn't break stride. "No one asked for your thoughts, James, as lofty as you think they are. And aren't you off duty?"

"At least consider my diagnosis—"

The nurses continued to wheel Baxter to X-ray as Doc Moore turned on him. "This is my patient," he snarled. "Now get out of my way!"

With something close to despair, James watched the doctor spin around and disappear through the double doors leading to X-ray. After a momentary hesitation, he followed.

He was sitting in one of the front chairs in the waiting room when the same harried nurse burst out of one of the X-ray rooms and all but ran to the nurses' station. She picked up the phone. "Doc Moore requests an anesthetist and surgeon STAT for type A aortic dissection."

James straightened as the nurse paused on the phone at the commotion inside X-ray. Another nurse approached, shaking her head. "Cancel the request. He's gone."

Weariness descended on James and he closed his eyes, his head tipping back. There was no satisfaction in being right, just bone-deep anguish. Why couldn't Doc Moore have listened to him? If he had, Baxter might at least have had a fighting chance.

James shivered, feeling a chill breath of air surround him like a kiss of winter. "May you rest in peace," he murmured.

The coldness abruptly lifted. His eyes flicked back open to find Doc Moore stumble from the X-ray room and give him a stare that roasted him with loathing . . . with accusation.

James stood, facing Doc Moore until the other man swung away and strode out of sight.

There was nothing James could do for Baxter now. As he walked out of X-ray, anger and guilt quickly replaced the anguish in his heart.

Doc Moore had highlighted exactly how intolerant some doctors were of anything not by the book, of anyone not with twenty years experience under their belt. Only, in this case he'd let his personal regard sway his professional duty of care.

On the drive back home, James was only half aware of the dark storm clouds building on the horizon, heralding a brewing thunderstorm. His natural high of the last few days had all but dried up, leaving him low, empty. And bewildered by the arrogance of many of the doctors he encountered.

They were supposed to put patients first, not their egos.

He blew out a breath. He was such a hypocrite. He'd been just as arrogant in his cockiness. A typical Bowheart. Josie was stronger than he was. At least she had the guts to stand up for what she believed in.

Guilt ate at him over Baxter's death. If he'd got there sooner . . . if he'd listened, really listened, to his subconscious . . .

Who was he kidding? He didn't believe in all this Josie-vision-voodoo stuff, did he? He could hardly be blamed for the death of some . . . stranger, dying of unknown complications in his bed. Could he?

Once home, he took a long, hot shower. When he got out, he could hear Rocco howling, long, drawn-out yowls that had his skin prickle with goose-bumps.

A death tribute?

He's just missing Marina, you fool.

After dressing, he grabbed his wallet and thrust it into his jacket pocket. Once next door, he refilled Rocco's water, trying not to think about how empty the house felt without Marina's warm presence.

He wanted her in his life. He needed her in his life.

Baxter's sudden death had only reiterated how short life was, and how easily one could live to regret the opportunities they'd missed by not listening to their heart.

Promising Rocco some doggie chow when he returned from his visit to Marina at hospital, James strode to his car. Firing up the engine, he reversed out the drive and then headed to a jeweler, a tiny shop renowned for quality craftsmanship and design.

Next stop, a florist.

Making a mental note to arrange a small arrangement for Baxter's upcoming funeral, he selected a dozen long-stemmed roses for Marina. Even after death, life went on. Baxter may have passed away, but a new life had been begun.

Alexander James.

Eagerness to see Marina and her baby had him push aside the negatives filling his head. And as he rode the elevator up to maternity, he admired the big, old-fashioned blooms in their silver cellophane. He smiled, remembering Marina's interest in the roses at Karlcodi's gardens.

She'd loved these roses. Red for passion, white for purity and elegance. His smile tilted into a wide grin. He'd best be careful lest Marina accuse him of becoming a romantic!

The doors pinged open. He strode through, down the corridor, and past the nurses' station, suddenly aware for the first time in days he felt . . . clean.

He rounded the open doorway to Marina's room, and froze.

She lay in bed, her wide eyes glued to the man leaning over her bed, a huge floral arrangement in his grasp. The man kissed her on the mouth and pressed the flowers into her hand. Turning to the mobile crib, his coarse voice filled the room. "There's my boy."

James must have said something audible, must have made some sort of involuntary protest, because suddenly Marina turned towards him, along with the man standing by her side.

He registered the deep, ugly scar embedded along one side of the man's jaw, registered the man's glittering, maniacal stare. Registered Marina's shocked denial.

"James, no. It's not what you think—"

Then somehow he was forcing his legs into action, spinning away to beat a hasty retreat out of the room, away from the mother and son who'd brought him back to life, and who he wanted with something too close to desperation.

He'd been such an idiot. A screw up. A so-called medical genius whose personal life was a war zone.

Clearly he didn't do relationships. He should already have known he didn't do happy families.

The flowers tipped over, the soft petals brushing against his leg as he marched like a defeated soldier down the corridor.

He followed a robust, uniformed lady into the elevator as she lugged a trolley with cleaning paraphernalia on board. He leaned his head against the back wall as they descended, hardly seeing the flashing numbers until the doors pinged open.

He stepped out after the cleaner and her rattling trolley. He stilled. Wrong floor. He hardly cared. He was numb to almost everything but the lancing pain in his chest.

So this was what a broken heart felt like?

The doors pinged shut behind him. A nurse looked up from her station as he loitered indecisively near the doors.

"James, hey!"

Stevie. Of course, he thought dully. It would be Stevie.

He nodded and forced his legs to move.

"Tom said you'd call soon." She studied him as he drew close. "Are you okay?"

"I'm fine, just . . . great."

"You bought me flowers?" she squeaked, a big smile brightening her face and clearly having her forget everything else.

He lifted the beautiful, delicate roses. They belonged to Marina. He shrugged, ignoring the deep ache in his heart. "Yeah, sure."

"They're beautiful! Thank you!"

All but jogging around her workstation, she threw her arms around his neck. In a furtive whisper, she said, "I've got a little something for you, too."

Still pressed against him, her arms slithered free. One hand slipped into her uniform pocket and retrieved what she was looking for. Before he'd even the foresight to step away, she was pushing a blister packet into his pants pocket.

"You can thank me later." She giggled, a wicked glint in her eyes.

As she moved behind her workstation again, he snapped out of the fog of his own self-pity and shook his head. He pushed a hand into his pocket to retrieve the drugs. "I don't think you under—"

"James!"

At the professor's voice, he pulled his empty hand free and stepped towards the other man, out of Stevie's earshot.

The older man gave him a questioning smile, making James immediately wonder what the professor had seen.

"Congratulations!" The professor abruptly pulled him in for a brief bear hug, apparently shrugging off suspicions. His eyes crinkled. "I'm going to visit the new Mom shortly." His eyes dulled just a little. "Robyn probably won't make it. Not just yet. I hope you understand."

Relief that the professor had chosen to trust him had him put aside his own problems, if only temporarily. "Of course." James put a hand on the older man's shoulder, "I understand."

"Thanks, son. Never mind. We've been blessed already in so many other ways."

James watched the professor move away, feeling a dark piece of envy burn him within.

He turned to Stevie, his hand burying back into his pocket to return her 'gift'. Only, she was nowhere to be seen.

Sudden, hysterical laughter bubbled up from the deep well of his soul, but he held it together as he walked out of the hospital and into the car park. He fired the BMW's engine. "Don't lose it now," he muttered. "Hold it together, for Josie's sake."

His stare immediately rested on her book. With a hoarse expletive, he leaned over to retrieve it. He sprayed open the pages before stopping somewhere in the middle, choosing a random poem in the same way his sister would.

He cranked up the CD player and allowed classical music to fill the car. Balancing the book on the steering wheel, he started to read.

That reflection is not me,
The water droplet gliding across my hand,
The wealth of lines and furrows spanned
Anyone can see that reflection isn't me . . .
But are my eyes crying silent tears?
Brimming inexcusably with all my whispered fears?
Is this me? Held within the tension of a single drop of water,
My image reminiscent of a lamb led to slaughter . . .
But I was strong, wasn't I? My body flexed towards the funnel of the sky—
That fantastic feeling that I'm never going to die!
So why, why do I gaze at my fingers, damp where a runnel of moisture lingers—
What changed?
What spark in my soul has been rearranged?
~Sue Allen

Raising his head, he caught sight of his face in the rearview mirror. He flipped the mirror up. The pain glazing his eyes was too raw, too real . . .

*

Oh, James.

Marina crumpled onto the pillows behind her as she watched the man she loved walk away.

Roger diverted his attention from Alexander, who lay sleeping peacefully in his crib, and with a smirk sarcastically murmured, "Poor James."

She frowned, too wrung out to even hate Roger just then. Besides, hate was such a black emotion, one she didn't want to carry around in her heart. "How do you know James?" she had to ask, hearing the weariness in her tone, the hint of resignation.

"Oh, I've made it my business to know everything about your life—your new life—boyfriends included."

A surge of fear pushed aside fatigue like a shot of adrenaline. "You've been stalking me?" She'd sensed him in the yard the other day and had experienced odd, unsettling feelings in her belly a handful of other occasions. Pity she'd not fully perceived her intuition.

He clucked his tongue and shook his head, his tone derisive. "Now, now. I never said that."

Marina closed her eyes, feeling the nightmare that was her ex-husband pressing into her mind. He hadn't been this monster when they'd first married. No, he'd hidden that dark side of himself until it'd been too late.

Her lids flicked open. He was still there. This couldn't be happening to her now! She'd started a new life in which to happily raise her child, and the man before her wasn't part of it. She was only glad he'd signed the divorce papers when he'd been too high to register his possessive streak.

She had a baby to protect now. "I want you out," she said softly, but her voice was pure steel. "Out of the hospital, out of my life. You're not welcome to visit me anymore and I'll do anything in my power to see you don't come near me again."

Roger's expression hardened, his insolent stare traveling slowly, possessively, up and down her body in its blue lacy nightdress. His nostrils flared. "I'm the father of your child. I have rights."

"Then I'll see you in court."

His lips thinned. A pulse throbbed to life at his temple. "Have you forgotten what I'm capable of?"

Never. Not when that fear still had the power to at times steal into her dreams.

"Marina, is everything okay?"

With a surge of profound relief, she turned towards the professor as he approached. "Professor. Ah, yes. Yes, I think so."

Roger arched a brow, sneering, "Never fear, I was just leaving." He paused at the end of her bed, and, giving her an insincere smile, he added, "I'll be seeing you."

Her shoulders slumped as she watched her ex finally leave the room. Seconds later, big fat tears rolled down her face. "I'm sorry," she gasped. "It was just such a shock seeing him here like this. I thought he was out of my life, a part of my past. I guess I was wrong."

The professor sat on the edge of her bed and drew her into a hug that would have given her comfort at any other time. Right then, all she imagined was her ex-husband taking his revenge.

"Now don't you go being sorry. You're a strong, spirited woman and a match for any man."

She sniffled. "I guess you're right."

The professor drew back and smiled down at her. "Trust me in this."

She managed a somewhat wobbly smile. "Okay."

He nodded, and then turned his attention to the portable crib. "Ah, here's the little fellah who couldn't wait to see the world." He chuckled. "He'll have James wrapped around his finger in no time."

Marina chewed her bottom lip. "Speaking of James . . . would you mind doing me a favor?"

The professor swung his attention back to her, his brow furrowed with concern. "Of course." He rubbed his gray-whiskered chin contemplatively. "Is everything okay?"

"The man who just left . . . he's my ex-husband." Her bottom lip trembled. "And he's . . . very bad news. I'm afraid for James."

"I see."

"Not only that, I think James might have misunderstood the situation when he came to visit me."

"You want me to check up on him?"

"Yes. Please."

He nodded, glancing at the wall clock. "I was finishing my shift in a few hours anyway. I'll swing by and make sure he's okay."

She smiled, but still felt unsettled, almost hollow inside. She might not have psychic ability, but more than once her woman's intuition had served her well. "I hope I'm not putting you out."

The professor stood, a tower of strength and humility. "I'm taking my wife out for dinner tonight. It's our fifteenth wedding anniversary." As she started to voice protest, he put up a hand and said, "Now don't you get anxious. She'd chew my ear off if I didn't go see James first."

Alexander stirred, then immediately started to wail. She went to him, cuddling him close and breathing in his distinct baby scent. She turned back to the professor. "I'm so glad James has you and Robyn as friends. Some of his mates have not been a good influence for him. He's had some . . . issues lately he's trying to overcome."

The professor nodded, visibly troubled. "Drugs. Yes, I suspected as much."

Chapter Six

Karlcodi Mental Hospital
Thursday, March 17th

Doctor Leonard flicked his pen over and over in his hand, staring sightlessly out the window of his hospital office.

Sarah Jane, his only child, his angel, missing now a little over four years. The hope he'd kept burning in his heart that she'd be returned to him had dimmed now to a barely audible flicker of light.

Deep in his heart he'd almost come to accept she was dead. But it was the 'what if's?' that gnawed away at a person's vitals, the same 'what if's?' that had eventually sucked all the love from his marriage.

He put the pen down and tore another doughnut in half from the take-out box on his desk. He pushed the half circle into his mouth and chewed without really tasting it, finding little joy to be had consuming yet more calories.

His mind was already drifting away, almost four-and-a-half years before.

Sarah Jane had been so beautiful. So full of life.

He remembered the afternoon he last saw her as though it was yesterday. He remembered the pride and fierce paternal love as he watched his daughter float down the stairs of their family home in her high heels. Her formal graduation dress had been the same fuchsia color as her flushed cheeks. Her long hair the color of sunshine had been swept up into some sort of elaborate do.

He and his wife had exchanged a look that only parents living in that perfect moment could explain. Their daughter had finished her senior schooling at the top of her class. And the night in front of her was hers to enjoy before going onto university and her dreams of becoming a marine biologist.

The world had been her oyster.

He swallowed, the doughnut becoming a thick lump traveling too slowly down his throat. He gulped down some strong black coffee, holding back the flood of tears with the festering wound that Josie had unwittingly reopened.

He recalled her chilling words with a masochistic ache that was almost welcome.

A murderer came to me. I know where his victim is buried. A young girl with a butterfly-shaped birthmark on her shoulder. Sarah Jane.

With shaky hands, he dragged out the handwritten notes he kept in a file reserved exclusively for Josie. He had files for all his patients in a special cabinet, but it was only hers that he kept in the locked drawer of his personal desk.

Out of all his patients, she bewildered and unsettled him the most. The things that came out of her innocent yet complex mind too often sent alarm bells off in his brain.

It was impossible she'd know where his daughter was buried, and yet . . . if there was even a ghost of a chance that she knew something . . . anything, she offered him—and his ex-wife—a chance of closure, of restitution, and the ability to say goodbye to their precious and adored only child.

He thudded a fist onto the desk, made breathless with a sudden attack of rage. It was wrong . . . wrong of him to allow a patient to have such a personal effect on him. *Damn it!* He should be used to it by now, should be stronger.

His face burned, but he reined in the rage that had galloped out of control. It was hardly his fault Josie dared to taunt him with such ludicrous claims!

Almost involuntarily, he turned to the framed photo of his daughter, a sudden calm descending over him. Sometimes the pain of seeing her happy face was too much and he'd place her portrait in his desk drawer. But more often than not it sat in pride of place on top of the desk, so that he'd never forget how much he loved her. How much he missed her.

Filled with a renewed sense of purpose, he trawled through the opened file and his notations, grasping at whatever it was that niggled at his subconscious. If nothing else, he'd at least reconfirm Josie's mental instability.

"I remember these drawings," he muttered, shuffling through the three he'd kept, one after the other.

He'd first met Josie eight years ago when he'd taken over as head psychiatrist. She'd refused to trust him, refused to speak. Yet in every one of their one-on-one sessions, she'd drawn for him. The same picture over and over until he'd grown almost bored by her persistence.

Goose-bumps sprung to life underneath his too-hot, too-tight suit jacket.

He took another, harder look at the first drawing. It was crude and child-like and totally unlike anything he'd seen of Josie's recent art skills. When she wasn't in regression, she had beautiful handwriting and a deft hand in art.

He flicked through the other two with a frown. They were indistinguishable except for just one or two minor additions to each one. He frowned. Damn it! Why hadn't he kept them all?

Each one had the same wobbly oval shape depicting an area of interest. Perhaps something from her childhood? The first one in his collection showed a row of oversized flowers that were child-like in their simplicity. The next she'd drawn what appeared to be a garden rake and spade, the last picture revealing a box . . . perhaps a house with a small 'x' and a squiggle of letters.

He inhaled with a wheeze, his eyes going wide. How could he have been so stupid? It was obviously a childlike treasure map, he squinted, with an 'S' or perhaps a number five, and beside it the letter 'J'.

Incredulity socked him in the guts. The drawings fell from his fingers and fluttered across the desk.

Was it possible Josie had written the initials SJ? Sarah Jane! His mind grasped the thought tight, desperate for affirmation. Was it possible?

He rolled his chair back and lurched to his feet. He had to see Josie, had to rule out all chance.

He heard the strains of a violin floating down the corridor long before he discovered Josie in her room, playing the instrument with her eyes squeezed closed in silent rapture.

He watched her play through the window of her door, for just a few seconds taken aback by her talent. Then he was pushing through her door and loudly clearing his throat.

Her eyes jerked open. Her bow stilled on the strings. She placed the instrument carefully onto the bed before she looked up and faced him, waiting.

Anger surged to life within. When wasn't Josie constantly testing his authority? Drugs were far and away the only thing that helped keep her in line and submissive.

He felt his jowls quiver as he asked, "Who gave you permission to play that here?"

Her chin tilted higher. "I need permission?"

"As your primary doctor I'm accountable for your health and your recovery. Of course you need permission."

"Well then," she gave an almost imperceptible nod, "do I have it?"

Her directness left him floundering.

Then her head tilted to the side. "But you didn't come here about my playing music, did you?"

He pushed his shoulders back, ignoring the strain on his jacket as he said, "As a matter a fact, I didn't. I came to ask about the maps you drew some years ago."

"Maps?" Her confused expression wasn't forced.

Damnation. Why had he come here? To inflict more self-pain? He'd not only lost his daughter, but his wife, too. Six months ago Emily had walked away from their marriage.

She'd been unable to bear living inside the bricks and mortar that was no longer a family home. Her words, not his.

Right or wrong, he was here now. And he wanted answers. "Years ago you sketched maps for me, one after the other. You don't remember?"

"I do, vaguely," she conceded, frowning a little. "But it was seven or eight years ago at least and . . . and I wasn't really myself. Molly helped me draw them."

Seven or eight years! The last glimmer of hope withered and died inside. Fool! Of course it had been that long. He'd just been thinking how she'd drawn for him all those years ago. Well before his daughter's disappearance.

"Right." He nodded stiffly, caring less that she wouldn't know what the hell he was going on about, "I guess that's it then."

Suddenly he wanted out of the room and away from Josie. Away from her too-perceptive stare. Spinning on his heel, he strode as fast as his tree-trunks for legs could carry him.

"Doctor."

He paused at the door.

"You were right to come. Sarah Jane hasn't yet found peace."

*

James pushed through Karlcodi's double doors with a heaviness pressing all around him. He was living and breathing, functioning even, but dead inside.

His career was no longer enough to sustain him; it never had been. He'd been surviving life, not living it. He knew that now.

He paused at the empty corridor stretching ahead, and swayed like a drunk. What the hell? His ears rang while everything ahead flickered in and out of focus, the corridor a dark, distorted tunnel.

His heart thrashed, his throat drying even as sweat beaded his brow. The soft, tinkling notes of tinny, familiar music sounded. Of course! "Somewhere Over the Rainbow".

The music box chime grew louder as—like a radiant light—a young woman floated towards him from the dark tunnel. Her long golden blonde hair fluttered around her, though there was no breeze.

He couldn't move. He was hypnotized, his legs leaden. And though he was terrified, he was also drawn, fascinated, despite himself.

"James." She was meters away, and yet the voice whispering in his ear conveyed her aching sadness and confusion. "You can see me. At last."

"Who are you?" he managed, the ability to speak a monumental effort.

"Tell Daddy to let me go." Her beautiful face contorted with grief and gave her the appearance of a young girl as she echoed softly, "Tell Daddy to let me go."

"James, it's me, Dr. Leonard."

He blinked. Dr. Leonard was snapping his fingers in front of his face. The loud tinkling notes ceased playing, the tunnel and the woman disappearing like they'd never been.

"Are you okay?" Leonard asked. "You look like you've seen a ghost."

The doctor hadn't been the only one to tell him that of late.

James dragged his hands over his face, feeling sick and foolish. Did he, too, belong in this hellhole with his sister and all the other patients? It seemed as though he'd been dragged to some psychotic level of madness he couldn't escape. "Sorry," he muttered abstractedly.

"I've just come from seeing Josie," the doctor went on, clearly deaf to James' apology, "and if it's not a bad time, I'd really like to talk to you about something."

James dragged his attention to the big man, and even in his state of disbelief, he found himself startled by Leonard's haggard appearance. The doctor had always been obese and unhealthy, but right then he looked like death. He looked how James felt.

He forced a nod, though it felt like a gesture of defeat. "Sure."

Minutes later, he was seated at the doctor's desk, looking over the trio of childlike maps. "Are these Josie's?"

Leonard nodded. "Yes."

"I'm not sure what it is you think I should be seeing?" he said dully, already losing interest. Everything paled alongside the day he'd experienced so far.

"I wondered if you might recognize any of the landmarks Josie has drawn here, maybe from your childhood?" Leonard gave an encouraging smile, but James was aware of the desperation behind it even before the doctor added, "Do those initials mean anything to you?"

James turned back to the pictures. He squinted at the one with the letters. "Looks like an 'S' and a 'J'."

"Yes, that was my interpretation, too."

James swung to him, and as he saw the doctor glance towards the framed portrait of his daughter, comprehension dawned. "Wait. You don't believe—"

If possible, the other man's face grayed further. "See, that was my reaction at first, too. I didn't want to believe, either. Didn't want to get my hopes up." His big shoulders lifted. "But right now Josie is all the hope I have in finding my missing daughter."

James inwardly reeled as he stared at the framed print of Sarah Jane. In retrospect the girl in the hallway didn't look much different to the girl in the photo. Just more . . . sad . . . lost.

James closed his eyes and put his hand up. "Stop. Please."

I'm not sure how much more I can take of this.

He heard the other man gasp in an indignant breath, knew grief was clawing at the other man with insidious fingers, but he couldn't swallow any more of this supernatural stuff, not right now. He'd had a lifetime of it.

He released a slow, calming breath before opening his eyes and flicking the doctor an apologetic look. But Leonard wasn't taking much notice of him anymore. The other man's face was streaked with moisture, and he was silently, openly sobbing.

"I apologize," James croaked, awkward and despairing. "I never meant any offense."

"She . . . was . . . my . . . baby," Leonard said between great wracking gulps of air, "with everything . . . to . . . to live for."

"I don't know what to say," James said quietly. What could he? Anything he had to offer would be trite, meaningless. He only wished he hadn't been so rude. So heartless.

The doctor looked up, smudging his red eyes on the end of his suit jacket sleeves before managing, "I guess I needed that." On another weary breath, he continued. "Thanks for not running off the moment I started blubbering. God only knows I would have in the same situation."

"If there's anything I can help with—" James put his hand up and let it fall back down onto the arm of his chair. "—anything at all." He paused, looking around the office lined with psychology books as the jingling notes of a music box resumed once more, faint but audible.

The doctor shook his head before James could utter another word. "I know it sounds crazy, I guess it is crazy to think these drawings would have anything to do with my Sarah Jane. It just seemed too much of a coincidence and I guess, well, I was probably being irrational, emotionally driven. I hope you can excuse me."

James nodded, admitting on a sigh, "Can you hear the music?" At Leonard's frown, he conceded, "No. Then I guess we're both going mad."

Leonard peered out of his bloodshot eyes, now even smaller in his fleshy face. "Don't hold back. I need to hear whatever is on your mind." He scraped a hand over the receding hairline of his brow. "I mean, you believed you saw something unusual on Josie's tape, didn't you? I admit I'm starting to see things in a different light now. There has to be more out there, doesn't there?"

Leonard, a believer? James inwardly shook his head. It seemed the doctor was prepared to accept whatever it took to help get him closure and stop the grief. All well and good, only, what if everything James had seen and heard was all his imagination? After the day he'd had he wasn't in any position to be judgmental.

He looked into the doctor's eyes, compassion taking hold. "Earlier in the corridor, you said it looked like I'd seen a ghost."

"Yes."

"I can't say for sure what I saw, what I heard." He dropped his gaze from Leonard's widening stare. Somehow disturbed by the sugarcoated, half-eaten doughnut in its box on Leonard's desk, he looked back up and pressed on. "But I think I saw a young, blonde woman, just moments after 'Somewhere over the Rainbow' started to play."

The doctor jerked to his feet. "Sarah Jane." He turned and ambled like a much older man to the window, gazing out over the rose garden.

Even with Leonard's back to him, James somehow knew the tears were now rolling hard and fast down the doctor's face.

On a choked breath, Leonard said, "Her last birthday I bought her an expensive music box from Tiffany's in New York, you know, to make up for all the hours I spent away from her. She hated it. My wife told me so after Sarah Jane went missing. Apparently all she ever saw was that little wind-up ballerina, trapped inside the box, all alone."

Leonard swiped his face with a sleeve. "All my psychological knowledge and training never once served me in seeing the pain of those closest to me, those I loved."

He shook his head. "No, all my time and energy was spent rescuing everyone else. I just . . . I just wish I'd spent more time with Sarah Jane. Stopped and . . . and seen things through her eyes."

The doctor turned back then, his expression turning fierce, resolute. "I'll do anything—" His voice cracked. "—anything to say goodbye."

James' emotions were seesawing off the charts. He felt powerless, like someone freefalling without a parachute, his anxieties fed by an addiction that was starving for a chemical hit.

Face it, he thought savagely. He'd already hit rock bottom the moment he'd seen Marina kiss the father of her child. And now the world had gone completely topsy-turvy. Never in his lifetime would he have imagined this straight-laced, logical doctor uttering such illogical thoughts, and asking him for advice . . . on what?

Helping spirits cross over?

It was crazy!

Leonard charged forward, re-animated as he took hold of the pages. "We have to take these maps to Josie, try and get her to remember the area she sketched to see if they really do relate somehow to my daughter's disappearance. They must have some sort of significance for her to have repeatedly drawn them."

"I'm not sure that's such a good idea."

Doctor Leonard's stare hardened. "Off the record, of course."

When they found Josie in her room minutes later, she was standing at her window, looking through the bars outside. "I know why you're here," she said, yet to turn and see who her visitors were. "It's all so clear to me now. I know what he wants."

James forced his gaze away from the violin—Marina's violin—laying in its opened case on the bed. He frowned, reining in his scattered thoughts at her reference. *"He?"*

Josie's gaze remained steadfast out the window. "Yes. Sarah Jane's murderer. He was in the room the other day. You saw him, too, James."

James found himself nodding to her back, but still inwardly denying it, trying to understand, trying to justify it somehow.

Leonard said in a choked voice, "We have the maps you drew. If you could try and remember some more?"

"It was the hospital ground. Always the hospital ground. Sarah Jane is buried here." She waved an arm to the grounds outside. "Stuck there, right there under that utility shed."

In his peripheral, James saw the doctor immediately cast a look at the maps. Then the doctor looked back up, shaking his head.

"No, no. You're confused, Josie. That's where our gardener hung himself."

"Yes, that's him," Josie agreed. "He killed himself in the same shed he buried Sarah Jane." She turned to them then, her eyes pained, haunted. "Timothy is her murderer."

The doctor stiffened beside him, and James was only too aware of his barely audible wheeze of breath.

"Timothy Doore? Impossible. Sarah Jane's grave . . . No. No. Impossible," Leonard repeated, swaying on feet that appeared glued to the floor.

"Not impossible." Josie's stare moved to rest on something . . . someone in the corner of the room. James dared not follow her gaze. "Timothy says he's . . . sorry."

James somehow found his voice past the horrible lump in his throat. "I think perhaps we should discuss this later. Doctor Leonard needs to sit down."

"No!" Josie's face paled, stark white, her attention swinging wholly to him. "James, don't leave now." Her fingers plucked at her shirt. "The energy has been building, James. It's all wrong . . . all bad. I don't want you to die! It's going to happen soon and I don't know if we can stop it."

James shuddered, aware he was a pinhead away from being violently sick. He thought back to the footage Leonard had shown him, Josie's words echoing in his mind like a hex he couldn't shake.

James won't die. He won't!

He swallowed hard, before reprimanding, "What have I told you about saying stuff like that? It scares people for nothing. Damn it, you're scaring me."

He turned to the doctor. "Let's go."

*

Leonard stumbled alongside James as he led him out the corridor.

He was so very grateful to James for getting him away from Josie, even as somewhere deep inside he was incensed. He'd had the perfect opportunity to delve further into Josie's psyche and test her sincerity before she regressed.

The bereaved stupor he'd kept locked away inside these last four years had long since become toxic with bitter resentment and lost hope. Now those dark emotions threatened to spill free and poison anyone within reach.

By the time James led him into his office, Leonard managed to contain his grief. It was as if he could feel Sarah Jane's presence as he marched over to the filing cabinets and unlocked the door.

His daughter needed him.

Flicking through the endless rows of patient notes inside, he muttered, "Here it is," pulling a file free and slamming the drawer shut as he read the name on the manila folder. "Timothy Doore."

He peeled back the cover with trembling hands, then read his handwriting aloud. "Patient deceased January twenty-third, two thousand and eight. Date of birth, twenty-seventh October, nineteen-seventy. Severe paranoid personality disorder. Responded positively to treatment and showed easy rapport with staff. No violent tendencies noted since admission."

He dropped the file onto the desk with a savage curse, and then rubbed an outspread hand through his thinning hair. "It doesn't add up."

Leonard turned to James. "To be honest, it seems far too convenient that Josie suggest my daughter was hurt by someone I knew, even trusted."

He sank into his chair and closed his eyes. Then immediately froze as an image hovering in his subconscious crystallized into startling, vivid life . . . thrusting him back in time, to four years earlier . . .

Leonard scarcely noticed the cloudless, turquoise sky through his windshield, or the lush sweep of lawn either side of the private road where a small mob of kangaroos grazed.

His thoughts were on his wife, Emily. He'd left her behind still fretful over Sarah Jane's failure to return home from her graduation night.

He gave a weary nod to the security guard manning Karlcodi's checkpoint gates, his belly churning.

As the parents of an only child, he understood full well his wife's concerns. But he'd tried to put her mind at ease.

More than likely Sarah Jane was at Sally's, her best friend's house. Sally's parents would already be at work, the girls alone and no doubt oblivious to the constantly ringing phone after their late night out.

Already two hours late for work, he'd been only too glad to escape to Karlcodi, to his patients, and lose himself in someone else's anxieties.

The scent of freshly turned earth hit his nostrils as he climbed out of his stately old Holden Statesman. The hospital was finally getting the shed they needed.

The earth-moving machinery had already left, but he could see Timothy Doore with shovel in hand, digging around the edges of the prepared ground.

"Hi, Timothy." He didn't wait for a response, his focus on the uncomfortable spin cycle in his belly. "You're doing a great job. Though aren't you digging a little deep for the footings?"

Timothy looked up, his gaze clashing a little defensively with Leonard's.

Leonard inwardly sighed. A past patient, while Timothy was now normal in many respects, he had never completely left behind his paranoia and distrust.

Timothy's stare dropped to the ground. "I wanted to make sure . . . wanted to make certain . . ."

Leonard shrugged away his explanations, dismissing the strange, queasy feeling in his gut before asking, "What's in the crate?"

Timothy resumed digging, his movements jerky, almost frenzied. He didn't look at Leonard as he said, "Pipes. Fittings. This and that."

Leonard nodded. "Okay. Sure. Good. As long as the books balance. I'm sure you know what you're doing." He smiled reassuringly. "I trust you."

Timothy froze. "No!" He shook his head wildly. "No, no, no, no! I don't want your trust." His eyes flashed loathing. "I don't want anything from you. No. Not anymore."

Leonard frowned at the other man's reaction, at the muscle jerking into life at Timothy's temple. He'd seen enough patients to know when irrational rage was leaping to the surface. He knew when to ease off.

"Fair enough." He took a couple of steps back. He really needed to think about Timothy's employment here. Really needed to look over the medical charts, perhaps reassess things. "If you want to have a chat, you know where to find me."

Leonard came back to the present with a violent start, his belly echoing the sensation of ill-ease he'd felt all those years ago—only a thousand times worse. "It was him."

*

James thrust open Karlcodi's front doors and all but stumbled outside. He tried not to think, not to feel. To do so hurt too much, pushed past the many boundaries of his rationale.

His leather shoes slapped out a rhythm on the concrete pathway through the front rose garden leading to the car park, his gaze somehow drawn to the plaque of Timothy Doore.

Was it even remotely possible there was some sort of life after death? If so, then what about the vision he'd seen of Baxter, a random patient, who had asked for his help? Even if his intuition was to be believed, then why had it let him down with his sister? His own flesh and blood?

Twenty-three.

He stilled at the number that came abruptly to him, clear as a bell in his mind.

He shook his head, brushing off the number, and his thoughts on the unexplainable mysteries of the universe. Was he keeping his mind busy to help keep at bay the memory of Marina and Alexander's father?

The cavity in his chest squeezed as he activated the keyless entry, the BMW lights flashing. Sliding into the driver's seat and mechanically clipping on his seatbelt, he fired up the engine to the sound of a radio DJ announcing, "And number twenty-three on this week's countdown . . ."

James flicked the off button, silencing the announcer. He breathed slow and deep, fighting for calm. He'd had the CD on, not the radio. What the hell was going on?

He turned in his seat, staring hard at Josie's poetry book. In all the emotional seesawing of the past twenty-four hours, he'd completely forgotten to take his present back to his sister . . . back to its rightful owner.

Twenty-three.

His breath hissed. He leaned forward and took hold of the book. Seconds, or was it minutes? later, he was flipping through the pages until he opened it to page twenty-three.

His heart stuttered.

I'm a dead man walking.
My bones are leaden,
Eyes deadened to all arrayed around me
In slow, lazy coils of nondescript delusion,
Adding to confusion—knotting up my brain . . .
And oh god, I'm so tired; so bitter. Things to be done
Littering my path in life so all I see is pain and strife.
Where'd the joy go? Where's the sigh of satisfaction
At a job well done? Life's a lousy slum . . .
Wrong place, wrong time; wrong decision, out of line
I'm heading down a cul-de-sac, wrong road, turn back.
I feel . . . what do I feel?
Numb
~Sue Allen

Chapter Seven

James didn't recall much of the drive home. He'd become immersed in the loud silence screaming in his head.

Carrying Josie's poetry book like it'd become an extension of himself, he unlocked the front door to his home, all too aware of the dark, empty house next door.

He stumbled inside, knowing there was no comfort to be found in the cold arms of reality.

Slamming the door shut behind him, he dumped his briefcase onto the floor. With a savage curse, he threw Josie's book across the room. Its pages fanned out as it skidded across the floorboards and slid to a stop in front of the liquor cabinet.

"Oh, hell." Dark emotion settled over him like a blanket. He sank onto his haunches, elbows on bent knees. His outspread hands covered his face, but failed to muffle his quiet, despairing sobs.

Nothing mattered anymore. Not Josie. Not Marina. Not even tiny, innocent Alexander.

He was a joke. A loser. A nobody who was slowly, quietly, going mad.

He had really started to accept the whole psychobabble bullshit his sister believed in with all her heart. He'd wanted to think he wasn't going crazy, wanted to think he wasn't seeing and experiencing things no normal person should.

He sucked in a deep breath, his back sliding down the cold, hard wall as he slumped to the floor. The foil in his pocket crackled like gunshot in his head, and his belly contracted with sharp need.

He pulled the packet free and through bleary eyes, he turned it over in his hands. Round and round, in time to the thoughts that spun through his mind and tangled more and more with each rotation.

The promise he'd made Marina echoed in his mind. *If there is any chance for us . . . I have to quit.*

But there wasn't any chance for them. She'd made her choice, and who could blame her?

With a hoarse laugh, he pushed four tablets out of their foil compartments. There were four more left. He freed the remainder, and with a sigh that was all weary resignation, he swallowed them all dry.

Within minutes, he could feel their effects crawling through his bloodstream. But it wasn't anything positive, or even relieving. He felt sick to his stomach . . . to his soul.

He was a recovering addict overdosing on the one thing that he once imagined had made him happy.

He staggered to his feet, the room spinning and lurching like a toy boat in a whirlpool. His laugh sounded like a jackal's.

He really was losing it, touched by the same insanity brush as his sister.

The colored liquor bottles drew his eye, beckoned him with their silent splendor. His loud guffaws edged too close with insanity, faded to gravelly, despairing sobs.

He found a glass in the cabinet and splashing in a good amount of aged malt whiskey, he raised it mid-air. "Here's to you, Dad."

He tossed back the amber liquid, feeling it burn like fire all the way to his belly. Swiping the tears from his eyes, he refilled his glass, and sucked down the drink in just a couple of gulps.

He felt woozy suddenly, uncoordinated. He staggered, his foot kicking the upended book. He cursed, bending down to retrieve it and focusing hard on the opened page even as the floor seemingly tilted, the walls spinning around him.

He held the book still, squinting to read.

Syllables of effervescent bubbles on your tongue
Letters chock a block with 't's—tempting, temptation;
Synonymous with the fate of Eve, who bit upon forbidden fruit
And wiped her wicked mouth upon her sleeve,
Burdened with remorse . . . but she was weak, of course . . .

So what of you? What will you do?
You'll never heed the hollow laugh as
Temptation sets her dainty hoof upon the path to tantalize and trip
you,
For you listen only to the monotone behind your skull.
'Feed your obsession' croons the whisper in your ear as
The long transgression into everything you fear begins.
Softly, softly speaks the voice
Assuring you your fateful choice is right and just
And can be trusted . . .
'Go on, just the once. It's not as if you're in the habit',
'No other person even knows—reach out and grab it'.
On and on the whisper goes
And your mind is full of snakes and ladders, lurching into right and
wrong
Lust dispels your indecision, guilt returns to parry blows
While the whisper on your shoulder knows
He's winning . . .
He's won!
And only now, do you realize just what you've done.
~Sue Allen

A piece of paper fluttered to the ground like a butterfly that had been trapped between the pages. Somehow he managed to retrieve it, to unfold it and register Josie's handwriting.

His eyes squinted once again, registering the words. He shook his head. "No. Way."

Two-twenty-three on the day they were wed,

Blue paint splattered red.

James Edward . . . dead.

He carefully folded up the page and tucked it into his pocket. Standing up, and suddenly feeling way too sober, he contemplated the bar and its menagerie of bottles.

He splashed another drink into his glass. He'd just have one more to fill the emptiness inside, to dull the chant of the words he'd read.

A baby wailed, an eerie echo in the thick, impenetrable fog surrounding him. The white haze abruptly dissipated, leaving a wall of mountain before him.

James looked all the way up, following the baby's cry. Marina stood on the cliff edge summit, gently shushing Alexander.

"Marina!" he yelled. But no sound came out of his mouth, even as he tried again, this time screaming her name.

His pulse thrashed. He felt something bad was about to happen, sensed the impending doom. He had to warn her! He started to climb, scrabbled desperately up the mountain, but his arms were too weak, his legs too heavy.

He heard a faint rumble that grew louder and louder, the earth trembling beneath him. The mountain began collapsing around him, the earth falling away.

He froze, gaping in disbelief as the bleached bones of, undoubtedly other victims who'd gone before him, were exposed. Huge rocks began to shift, then roll and bounce their way downward . . . but Marina and her baby seemed patently unaware of their rapidly shrinking platform.

Marina! No, no, no!

The earth gave way high above him, dislodging a boulder that immediately crashed its way down towards him. He couldn't move. He couldn't breathe.

Marina, I'm so sorry.

He saw nothing . . . nothing but darkness. Pitch black, veiling darkness.

Am I dead?

A white, dazzling light abruptly shone directly above him. He looked up, but couldn't bear to stare directly into its brightness.

He turned away, disorientated and confused. Only then did he notice the spiral of stairs beneath him, an endless round of steps disappearing into the darkness not lit by the white radiance above.

Where am I?

Heaven? Hell? Was it possible? Was he suspended between life and death? Good and evil?

As suddenly as the thought took hold, he started toward the stairs. He was drawn downward, sure and confident, his vision adjusting to the ever-dwindling light.

He paused. Just meters ahead another radiant light appeared, illuminating a beatific figure. But as he walked closer, the image quickly became something else entirely, a depiction of the true horror inflicted.

A human form . . . visibly beaten, wounded, his flesh hanging in bloodied strips, his skin forever scarred beyond anything humanly tolerable.

Jesus? It had to be! Dried blood streaked his gentle face, telling its own violent and graphic story from where a barbed crown of thorns had been forced onto his head, cutting through his scalp like razors. Yet warmth and compassion poured out from the Holy Spirit, embracing James with unconditional, undying love.

Despite this, James felt a powerful pull to continue his descent. As the apparition put out his hands, palms up, James remained silent and willful, comprehending the emotional plea pouring from . . . Jesus, but unable . . . unwilling, to cede.

My Child, I gave my life for you. I endured this suffering for you and your fellow man so that you may have life. Look me in the eye, believe in me, and accept my sacrifice. Follow me out of the darkness and into the light of life. Peace I leave with you. My peace I give you.

James wanted to heed the advice, and yet still he moved forward, brushing past the potent form while Jesus' words filled his head until he was dizzy with self-doubt.

He clutched hold of the rail, gasping. A vast black void took away the stairs beneath. And then, just as suddenly, revealed his near-lifeless form slumped below on the lounge room floor.

It struck him then. He was in hell . . . his own, private hell. It was time to make a choice.

"James, answer the door."

Professor?

He fell, the pit of his belly lurching with the sudden momentum as he slammed back into his body. He heaved in a breath, unable to move, unable to speak.

"I just wanted to make sure you were okay."

His mentor felt so close, yet his voice sounded so far away.

"I made a special detour here even though it's my and Robyn's anniversary."

"Leave me alone," James managed through a gritty throat. "Just . . . go." I don't want you to see me like this. I don't want your compassion. I especially don't want your sympathy.

"Well, I'll be catching up with you soon, one way or the other."

The professor's tread moved away as he called out, "No James Edward I know ever gives up."

The car door slammed, the Volvo's engine firing up.

Sudden comprehension dawned. James' heart froze, then beat into double-time. The professor's car was blue.

Blue paint splattered red.

"No!" His voice came out like someone yelling underwater. And still he couldn't move. "Oh, please . . . no." His head swam, but it had little to do with the chemical cocktail he'd swallowed.

With shaky hands, he tugged out Josie's handwritten note. He squinted until double vision became single, grasping the impossible, scarcely able to breathe as he read aloud, "Two-twenty-three on the day they were wed, blue paint splattered red. James Edward . . . dead."

James Edward Newton.

He shook his head. "No!" Then squeezed his eyes shut against the utter pain in his head. It was never himself! It was the professor. It was his blue car. It was his anniversary!

James looked at his watch. Two-twenty.

"Shit. Shit, shit, shit!"

He ripped his cell phone from his jacket pocket and pressed in the professor's number. He couldn't focus as panic robbed his fingers of all coordination. Finally, he made the connection.

*

The professor pushed on the accelerator a little harder. His protégée would be fine. James Bowheart was a genius in the making, and a caring, sensitive young man to boot.

Marina had already made a big difference in the young man's life. He only hoped James realized how truly lucky he was.

And so was he.

It was cliché, but Robyn was the best thing that had ever happened to him.

His life was complete. Well . . . almost. A beautiful wife, a brilliant career. The only thing Robyn wanted was the only thing he couldn't give her.

He'd give her anything, his life if need be, for her to hold their child in her arms. Some days the sadness, the yearning tearing at her voice almost killed him, yet still he'd never stopped believing, never stopped praying for a miracle of their own.

He felt his brow crease as he thought back to their earlier phone conversation.

She hadn't been angry at all he'd been delayed for their dinner. In fact she'd almost sounded excited. The present she had for him must be very special. His breathing hitched.

Was it possible . . .?

His cell phone chimed.

He didn't normally talk on the cell phone while driving, but it was probably Robyn. He'd quickly reassure her that he was on his way, then disconnect. No harm done.

Leaning over to where he'd tossed his cell phone earlier onto the passenger seat, he picked it up. "Hello." No answer. "Hello?" He glanced down at the screen for caller ID. "James?"

Movement in his peripheral screamed 'warning' a millisecond before he saw the sedan—its driver slumped over the steering wheel—heading straight for him.

He jerked his car hard to the left, the tires squealing as he instinctively hit the brakes. The other sedan clipped the tail end of his car, launching his vehicle sideward into the air—straight towards a line of huge eucalyptus trees edging the road.

Metal crunched inward as it impacted solid, immovable wood.

Robyn, I love you.

Air left his lungs as he was flung forward like a rag doll. Then . . . nothing.

Want more Awakenings stories by Mel Teshco and Kylie Sheaffe...

Homecoming

What will it take for doctor-in-training, James Edward Bowheart, to drop his pre-conceived beliefs and fully awaken to his innate psychic abilities? That believing in them might well have prevented the death of the professor—his good friend and mentor—has left James reeling. His sister, Josie, never once doubted in his surreal visions and messages, making him realize he owes it to himself—and to the memory of the professor—to at least explore what he consciously turned his back on.

With the love of his girlfriend Marina helping to shift his energy, James soon pieces together some of the hidden truths from his past. But will his soul searching deliver him the happily ever after he yearns for or will he be forever entwined with the visions that haunt him?

Homecoming available HERE[1]

---

1. https://books2read.com/u/38ywEL

Chapter One of Homecoming

Brighton, Australia

Monday, March 21st

Robyn Newton leaned into the toilet bowl and vomited again, her belly contracting involuntarily until the sickness finally passed.

My love, why were you taken from me?

She couldn't cry anymore. She'd cried every tear out in her body, and then some. She felt cold, empty, heartsick, and disillusioned. On top of it all, she'd been fighting a guilt that ate at her, piece-by-piece.

She should have told him.

But it was too late now. Her husband had been her universe, her soul mate, ripped out of her life by a drunk, hit and run driver.

She looked into the mirror. She was gaunt and hollow-eyed, her thin face haunted by the horror of the last five days.

A knock on the door sounded, followed by Marina's gentle inquiry, "Are you okay?"

Robyn took a second to respond. "Yes. I'll . . . I'll be right out."

"Okay. Take your time. I'll be waiting downstairs."

Robyn didn't answer. She was already sinking back into the quagmire of her bleak emotions, staring blankly into the mirror, waiting . . . waiting to be woken up from this nightmare.

How could he have been taken on their anniversary? How could he have been taken at all?

Her hands clenched, but she forced her trembling fingers open to adjust the collar of her lemon dress, her husband's favorite. He never had liked the color black.

She closed her eyes. It'd become a habit lately. Every time she blocked out the world, she saw her husband's face; his brilliant laughing eyes, the creases in his brow, his graying hair. But mostly, his love that had shone bright just for her.

Hugging her torso, she whispered, "I wish I could talk to you one more time, tell you how much I love you, how much I miss you. I wish I could explain how happy you made me, but mostly, I wish I could tell you that no one could replace you in my life."

She breathed in deep. The love he'd given her for so many years would keep her strong. For him, she could do this. Somehow.

Her lids flicked open as she expelled her breath. Retrieving her clutch purse from the sink, she walked slowly out of the en suite and into her bedroom, trying not to feel as the king-size bed loomed in her vision.

Leaving the main bedroom, she paused at the entrance of the study right next to the bedroom she'd shared with her husband. There had been many nights he'd burned the midnight oil in here, adding to his journal and reading. But he'd only ever been a room away.

Now . . . now he was unreachable. At least, in the physical realm.

Her husband's scent still lingered, and she inhaled the air until her breath caught on a sob. Hurrying to his big oak desk, she retrieved his bound leather journal.

She didn't have her husband with her anymore, but at least she had the book he'd poured his heart and soul into. That would have to be enough. Heartsick, she spun away with another sob and fled from the room, closing the door behind her with a sharp snap.

Some things hurt way too much, despite the yearning.

By the time she reached the stairs, her urge to hurry was fading fast. She didn't want to leave, didn't want to face the torment ahead.

As she made her way slowly downstairs, James and Marina stepped forward to meet her, assisting her down the last few steps. She really must look as fragile and vulnerable as she felt.

Too soon they were at the church, people crammed into the pews while others stood, with her husband's casket taking center stage, almost like his death was something to be celebrated.

In some distant place in her mind she took in many of the mourners who attended, doctors and nurses who had worked at the hospital with her husband, and many of his students. In one of the pews halfway down the aisle, their—*her*—elderly neighbors sat alongside a middle-aged lady who'd cut her and James' hair the last ten years.

There were so many others she didn't recognize, colleagues and admirers of her husband's work. People her husband had touched in some way.

Her nails dug into the palms of her hands as she sat at the front pew, Marina and James sitting either side.

She only half-heard the minister drone on about the virtues of James Edward Newton. But what did he understand of her husband? He was reading from his notes like he would a sermon. He didn't know her husband, had no idea how good, kind, and beautiful James really was. *Had been.*

Journal pressed tightly against her torso, she stood, ignoring the surprised looks from Marina and James, from the packed gathering who'd come to mourn her husband.

"You'd like to say a few words?" the minister asked.

"Yes." She nodded. "Yes, I would."

She'd never been fond of public speaking but now her fears seemed achingly trivial.

The minister moved away from the pulpit and allowed her to take over. She put the journal onto the lectern. The casket, with its huge wreath of flowers, drew her stare and she had to swallow past the lump in her throat before she spoke.

"I never got a chance to say goodbye to my husband," she began hoarsely. "I never really got a chance to thank him for everything he's done for me over the years." She swept a hand towards the casket, trying not to imagine her vibrant, wonderful husband lying dead inside, trying not to think about his broken body. "But now, I have my chance."

She was vaguely aware every person in the gathering was hanging onto her every word, many of them dabbing at their eyes. It meant little to her right then. She took a breath, taking a moment to gather herself. She looked skyward. "James, my love, you were my heart. You were my soul mate, my other half. I cherished every single moment we had together. Thank you."

She heard a collective sigh from the people on the pews. She looked downward, focusing on his journal. "I'd like to share a little something from him that very few of you would know."

Opening the first page, she read her husband's handwriting.

"I saw a miracle today."

She paused, choked up. She took another breath, and then continued reading.

"My colleagues and I advised a first-time mother to say goodbye to her prematurely born daughter. We were all medically aware the tiny girl's spark of life couldn't possibly last. The Mom refused to listen. She demanded to know how we could dare suggest such a fate—that we were not God. Instead, she channeled every ounce of her determination, every ounce of her love into her baby, her baby that she touched and held at every opportunity, despite being warned not to. There was no scientific explanation for how her baby responded and fought for her little life . . . She wasn't aware that it was impossible, she was surviving . . . Thriving, on the power of love. Love that my tired colleagues and I had underestimated, love that we should have offered ourselves. And hadn't. The mother sang words that were filled with love and rich with belief, words in which her baby responded. That is the kind of love that is not, and will never be, found in the barren space of a Humidicrib."

The writing blurred. Robyn looked up, memorizing the last few lines of her husband's scrawled handwriting as she finished aloud, "That was the defining moment for me, the start of much self-interrogation.

The questioning of what more I could offer in regards to scientific medicine."

An elderly gentleman a few rows back blew his nose into a large square handkerchief, but otherwise the silence was almost deafening.

Robyn closed the journal. Prisms of light poured through the stained-glass window overhead, depicting the birth of Jesus. She cleared her throat, fighting back raw emotion. "Five days ago my husband and I planned to celebrate our anniversary. Today I'm forced to say goodbye to a man who never knew he gave me something so precious, so long awaited. A miracle of our very own."

She imagined his loving face in heaven as she closed her eyes. "I was going to tell you that night. My darling. We're having a baby."

The church filled with surprised murmurs as she gathered up the journal and made her way down the two steps. She paused beside the gleaming, wood-grain casket. She laid a hand on it and whispered, "I love you." Tears flowed down her face, tears she'd mistakenly imagined were all cried out. "Goodbye, my darling."

*

James watched as the last of the mourners murmured their condolences to a pale but dignified Robyn before they trailed away from the professor's gravesite and to their respective cars.

He retreated a few meters, giving Robyn some space and time to grieve alone.

Grief snarled in his own belly, a sickness that threatened to swell. *Bloody hell.* How could Robyn stay so strong when all he wanted to do was scream, to rant and rave at the unfairness of it all?

Remorse hit him hard. If he hadn't given into the drugs, the professor wouldn't have come looking for him and would still be alive today. It should have been his last breath taken after the drugs he'd ingested, not the professor's.

He'd been at least partly responsible for taking away one of the world's top surgeons. And one of the finest men a person could hope to have as a friend.

The professor's accident had left a deep void inside him, but it had also given him a conviction he never knew he possessed.

No more drugs, no more self-defeating behavior. It'd taken the professor's death to make him see the light, to see life now as a gift and something to be treasured.

The professor's death would not be in vain.

It would take one step at a time, one day at a time to overcome his drug dependency. It might be too late to win back Marina, but he'd do this. For himself. For his sister.

The time off work had been a fundamental part of the healing process, not just with the professor's death, but his own emotional blockages. He'd thrown out his stash of pills and tipped the liquor from every bottle of alcohol down the sink.

He didn't need to prove to anyone, to himself, he was strong-willed. It wasn't necessary anymore. His pill popping and his one-time binge drinking had ended for good.

Marina walked towards him, following his lead. Her stare clashed with his, hurt all too apparent in her eyes. Her grief was easily evident, but he could also decipher other emotions: abandonment, betrayal, rejection.

His heart turned over. He knew how she felt. Even knowing she was with Alexander's father, he wanted her like nothing ever before.

James released a long, slow breath. Was Marina really lost to him? Life could be taken at any moment—the professor was proof of that. But he was a fighter, clean of drugs and ready to embrace life.

He had nothing to lose . . . and yet everything to lose.

Marina looked away, hiding her too-easily-read emotions. But he didn't apologize, not right then. Besides, Marina was sure to hate him even more once he explained the reason behind his long absence, the reason he'd ignored all her phone calls and locked himself in his house, away from the world and everything in it.

He turned, glancing at the headstones with their etched words. He shook his head. A mini-bio recounting a person's lifetime, a person with a mother, a father, a family. All their worth transcribed into a stone monument.

He was only glad he'd come to understand there was more to life than just what one could see.

"So sad," Marina said softly, her voice sounding little-girl lost. "Robyn and the professor . . . they were perfect for each other."

The trees cast shadows over the headstones farther away, and James wondered at the sudden prickle of foreboding as a man in the distance stepped behind a large tree.

He pushed aside the silly apprehension, his focus returning to Marina. She'd said very little to him since this morning, where a friend had dropped her off at Robyn's house at the same time he'd pulled into the driveway.

There was much explaining to do, but a funeral wasn't the time or the place.

A light breeze picked up Marina's hair, tugging at the strands she'd pushed back into a tight bun that was losing the battle of containment. The vibrant red-gold strands were a sharp contrast to her severe, knee-length, black dress flaring out from the waist.

She looked beautiful. But it was a different kind of beautiful. She looked untouchable, distant. And a little bit scared.

He stepped towards her, searching for a safe topic. "How . . . how's Alexander?"

"He's good. His healthy lungs keep me awake most nights." Her face was a tight mask that slipped just a little at the mention of her son. Even so, she radiated a tension that screamed, *back off.*

Becoming aware of the slightly dark shadows under her eyes, he nodded. "You do look a little tired."

She laughed, but the sound was hollow. "Believe me, I feel it."

He ached to take her into his arms, to soothe away the strain so visible on her face. But it was no longer his right. It had probably never really been his right. "At least you have Alexander's father there, helping out."

Damn, just saying those words made his tongue thick, like he couldn't speak English.

"Roger?" Her laugh raised another few decibels, one of her hands closing into a fist over the cross she wore on a silver chain around her neck. "I wouldn't let that man near my baby if he was the last person on the planet."

James' pulse stuttered, disbelief and hope crawling through the quicksand of sorrow. "He's at home with him now though . . . isn't he?"

"No." She shook her head, scattering more hair free from its pins. "No! I put a restraining order put on him right after his unexpected hospital visit. My aunt is with Alexander. She's staying for a month to help out."

Relief warred with anxiety. He'd been so consumed by his grief he hadn't even noticed Marina's aunt next door! "A restraining order? But I thought—"

"You thought wrong." Marina's bottom lip trembled. "The bastard's been stalking me."

A protective instinct rose inside like a powerful wave. He didn't ride the emotion. He backed off. He'd play it safe and smart, not act on his compulsions.

In his peripheral, he saw Robyn turn from the graveside and approach, her head tilted high and proud, dark sunglasses concealing her red-rimmed, bleary eyes. Her hands clasping the professor's journal to her bosom conjured a déjà vu moment that reminded him of Josie and her poetry book.

Fresh guilt lanced through him. His sister was yet another loved one he'd neglected since the professor's death.

He took hold of Marina's hands. "We need to talk."

She tugged free. "I tried that already. I rang . . . I left messages on your answering machine."

"I know." He wasn't going to make excuses. "Could I drive you home?"

Her bottom lip wobbled, as if all her pent-up emotions threatened to spill free. "Thanks, but I can find my own way."

He ached to kiss her mouth, to soothe away her fears and fatigue. To help make her forget what an idiot he'd been. Instead, he reluctantly stepped back, and a moment later, offered his arm to Robyn.

The older woman managed a wan smile. "You have both been so very kind to me. It means a lot. Thank you."

"We want to be there for you, whenever you need us," Marina said huskily, falling into step beside them.

Robyn stilled beside James' car and bowed her head. James knew she held back sobs. She lifted her chin, and with surprisingly steady hands she peeled the journal from her body, holding it out to James. "My husband considered you one of his closest friends. I know . . . he'd want you to have this."

Remorse and uncertainty hit James hard. He was so unworthy of the professor's life's work. "I couldn't."

A single tear trekked past her sunglasses and down her face. "I insist." She placed a hand over her belly. "We insist."

James shoved aside self-doubts, wanting only to reassure as he accepted the book. "Thank you. I'll treasure this journal and the words inside it."

She gave an almost imperceptible nod. "I know you will. I believe you'll continue on with his good works."

"You have my word."

"There's just one condition."

"Anything."

She dabbed away the tear with a crumpled tissue. "I'd like our child to have the journal, a keepsake when he, or she, turns eighteen."

"Of course. I'll keep it safe until then."

She managed a wan smile. "Thank you."

James opened the passenger door, then shut it behind Robyn with a clunk. At the uneasy sensation crawling down his spine he looked back, past the gravestones and to the trees, where the same man stood, too far away to see him clearly.

With a frown he turned to Marina, and froze. She was staring at the man, horror etched into her face. He stepped towards her, "Marina, are you okay?"

"It's him," she whispered starkly. "It's Roger."

Shit!

His instincts had warned him earlier. It seemed he still had a way to go in learning to listen and trust in them.

He looked back, scanning the area. But Roger was already retreating like a flickering shadow amongst the far-off trees.

James drew her into his arms, holding her close. "It's okay," he said. "He's leaving." The coward. "I won't let him hurt you."

Marina stepped back, her body stiff. "I wish I could believe you." She looked away as a car pulled in behind his BMW. "My ride is here. I best get back to my son."

Had he blown all chance of being with Marina? In the past week, he'd lost a true friend and probably the woman he loved. And as he watched her walk away he had to wonder if she was walking out of his life for good.

Some hour and a half later, with the professor's journal in hand, James unlocked the front door of his house and stepped inside.

He took a deep, calming breath, trying not to imagine the every goings-on next door as he faced the empty room, trying not to envision the love filling every pore of Marina's home as he entered the tome-like quiet of his own house.

Therein lay the difference. She had a home. He had a house.

He had cleared out what had once been his liquor bar. He didn't need to prove to anyone anymore that he wasn't his father. Now he used it to store his textbooks, medical encyclopedias, paperwork, and, temporarily, Josie's poetry book.

He put the professor's journal down beside the poetry book, unable to find the will to read it right then. Not even one word. His mentor's death was still too raw, too recent.

His reserves of strength could only take him so far.

Instead, almost abstractedly, he picked up the poetry book and strode over to the recliner near the window overlooking Marina's house. He flicked on the freestanding lamp nearby. He'd read a little and keep an eye on things next door.

He opened the book and thumbed through a couple of pages. "Perfect," he mused.

Be still my friend and believe . . . the steepest path—
Your treadmill of despair is passed.
The prayer seeded in a pit of misery is known
And strength to haul your burden has grown beyond the frailest shoots
To become a sapling, sinuous and strong—roots tapped deep into the warmth of love,
Branches spreading high above, in harmony and song . . .
For you, my friend, belong.
~Sue Allen

If you would like to know when Mel Teshco's next book is available, news, cover reveals and more, you can sign up for my newsletter: madmimi.com/signups/121695/join

Check out my website – http://www.melteshco.com/

You can also friend me on Facebook at https://www.facebook.com/mel.teshco

Or on my author Facebook page at https://www.facebook.com/MelTeshcoAuthor

And occasionally on Twitter at https://twitter.com/melteshco

Contact me: melteshco@yahoo.com.au

If you enjoyed our story we'd be delighted if you would consider leaving a review. This will help other readers find our books.

About the Authors

Mel Teshco loves to write scorching sci-fi and contemporary stories with an occasional paranormal thrown into the mix. Not easy with seven cats, two dogs and a fat black thoroughbred vying for attention, especially when Mel's also busily stuffing around on Facebook. With only one daughter now living at home to feed two minute noodles, she still shakes her head at how she managed to write with three daughters and three stepchildren living under the same roof. Not to mention Mr. Semi-Patient (the one and same husband hoping for early retirement...he's been waiting a few years now.) Clearly anything is possible, even in the real world.

Kylie Sheaffe once a burdened spiritual intuitive, Kylie has learned to embrace her inherited gifts, unleashing their healing capacity, extraordinary insights, and unconditional love. Being real and approachable with her quiet wisdom, she offers a world of unexplored potential.

Books by Kylie Sheaffe and Mel Teshco

Awakenings: series order

No Ordinary Gift

Believe

Homecoming

Books by Mel Teshco

Contemporary:

Desert Kings Alliance: series order

The Sheikh's Runaway Bride (book 1)

The Sheikh's Captive Lover (book 2)

Coming soon

The Sheikh's Forbidden Wife (book 3)

The Sheikh's Secret Mistress (book 4)

The Sheikh's Defiant Princess (book 5)

The VIP Desire Agency: series order

Lady in Red (book 1)

High Class (book 2)

Exclusive (book 3)

Liberated (book 4)

Uninhibited (book 5)

The VIP Desire Agency Boxed Set (all 5 books in the series)

Box sets with authors Christina Phillips & Cathleen Ross

Sheikhs & Billionaires

Taken by the Sheikh

Taken by the Billionaire

Taken by the Desert Sheikh

Resisting the Firefighter

Standalone longer length titles: (50k-100k)

Highest Bid

As I Am

Standalone novellas and short stories: (15k-40K)

Stripped

Clarissa

Camilla

Selena's Bodyguard (also part of the Christmas Assortment Box)\

Anthologies:

Down and Dusty: The Complete Collection

The Christmas Assortment Box
Secret Confessions: Sydney Housewives
Science Fiction:
The Virgin Hunt Games volume 1
The Virgin Hunt Games volume 2
The Virgin Hunt Games volume 3
Coming soon
The Virgin Hunt Games volumes 4-6
Dragons of Riddich: series order:
Kadin (free prequel - book 1)
Asher (book 2)
Baron (book 3)
Dahlia (book 4)
Wyatt (book 5)
Valor (book 6)
The Queen (book 7)
Alien Hunger: series order
Galactic Burn (book 1)
Galactic Inferno (book 2)
Galactic Flame (book 3)
Coming soon
Galactic Blaze (book 4)
Nightmix: series order:
Lusting the Enemy (book 1)
Abducting the Princess (book 2)
Seducing the Huntress (book 3)
Winged & Dangerous: series order
Stone Cold Lover (book 1)
Ice Cold Lover (book 2)
Red Hot Lover (book 3)
Winged & Dangerous Box Set (all 3 books in the series)

Dirty Sexy Space continuity with authors Shona Husk and Denise Rossetti:

Yours to Uncover (book 1)

Mine to Serve (book 6)

Ours to Share (book 8)

Standalone longer length titles: (50k-100k)

Dimensional

Mutant Unveiled

Shadow Hunter

Existence

Standalone novellas and short stories: (15k-40K)

Identity Shift

Moon Thrall

Blood Chance

Carnal Moon